RICH $AVAGE 2

Lock Down Publications and Ca$h
Presents
RICH $AVAGE 2
A Novel by *Martell "Troublesome"*
Bolden

Rich $avage 2

Lock Down Publications
Po Box 944
Stockbridge, Ga 30281

Visit our website @
www.lockdownpublications.com

Lock Down Publications
Like our page on Facebook: Lock Down Publications @
www.facebook.com/lockdownpublications.ldp
Cover design and layout by: **Dynasty Cover Me**
Book interior design by: **Shawn Walker**
Edited by**: Kiera Northington**

Stay Connected with Us!

Text **LOCKDOWN** to 22828 to stay up-to-date with new releases, sneak peaks, contests and more…
Thank you.

Submission Guideline.

Submit the first three chapters of your completed manuscript to ldpsubmissions@gmail.com, subject line: Your book's title. The manuscript must be in a .doc file and sent as an attachment. Document should be in Times New Roman, double spaced and in size 12 font. Also, provide your synopsis and full contact information. If sending multiple submissions, they must each be in a separate email.

Have a story but no way to send it electronically? You can still submit to LDP/Ca$h Presents. Send in the first three chapters, written or typed, of your completed manuscript to:

LDP: Submissions Dept
Po Box 944
Stockbridge, Ga 30281

DO NOT send original manuscript. Must be a duplicate.

Provide your synopsis and a cover letter containing your full contact information.

Thanks for considering LDP and Ca$h Presents.

Martell "Troublesome" Bolden

Chapter 1

A few nights after Gee's murder, there was a vigil being held in his honor. Most of everyone from the hood stood around the shrine, which was covered with teddy bears, flower bouquets, lit candles and a collage of flexed-up photos of Gee. And in the background, the DJ played Polo G's tune, "Losses."

Ace pulled up with Paris and Adonis, then parked his Acura curbside. Leaving him alone, Paris grabbed their son from the backseat, then exited. Ace took a deep breath to calm himself. Before stepping out of the car, he grabbed his .45 Glock with a thirty-two-shot clip, a converter switch from beneath the driver's seat, concealed it on his waist under his T-shirt depicting a photo of Gee's face. Walking up to the shrine, which was set in front of Mika's house, Ace sat down a bear with the rest of the memorabilia. He noticed his sister being comforted by friends and family, then made his way over to Mika and gave her a hug. She was bawling, while he was fighting back tears.

"Sis," Ace began gingerly, "I know this shit hard, but we gotta be strong for lil bro."

"I just miss him so much," Mika cried.

"Trust me, so do I. Why don't we go and talk alone?" He wiped away her tears.

"Alright."

Ace led the way to his Acura and pulled open the passenger door for Mika. He then walked around the car and stepped into the driver's seat. For a moment they sat in silence, not really knowing where to begin. Both of them looked out at all the people present on behalf of their lil brotha, and it made them realize just how much Gee was loved.

Ace noticed Chedda stood off to the side with Sly, Bookie and Poppa, who had Gee's pitbull, Beast-Mode, on a leash. Paris was out there with Adonis on her hip among the gathering, offering her condolences to some of Ace's family and friends. Reverend Johnson was among the crowd doing God's work. Kiki was there crying her eyes out, while Red and others consoled her. Ace noticed Stone and Star weren't there.

He partially believed Stone was responsible for sending those shooters at him that night. But thus far, he wasn't exactly sure of it, because he hadn't gotten any confirmation. And with all the beef Ace had in the streets, he couldn't exactly say for sure who was behind the shooting. But whenever he found out whoever it was, Ace vowed to make sure they stopped breathing.

"Look, I feel like what happened to Gee is all my fault," Ace said in a lowered voice, breaking the silence.

"No, it's not. When Glen chose to be in the streets then he accepted whatever fate came with that choice," Mika told him.

"But I was s'pose to be my brotha's keeper. Now I gotta do all I can to keep you safe."

"Don't worry so much about me, Ace. It's you who niggas want to kill, so it's your safety you need to worry about. Besides, I won't be staying in the hood for much longer. I'm moving out of town to Green Bay. What do you think about that?"

"Think it's good for you and my nephew. I'll make the drive out there to see y'all. Shit might be better for you there anyway."

"Maybe you should move there too."

"Sis, I ain't leavin' Milwaukee."

"You mean Killwaukee," she snorted.

8

"Whatever you wanna call it. I'ma stay here and just run it up until twelve or opps catch me slippin' in these trenches."

Mika peered at her lil brother and shook her damn head. "Ace, you don't have to go out like that," she replied, annoyed.

"Sis, I wish it wasn't like that, but it's a fucked-up lifestyle I'm involved in. I'd give anything for shit to be normal."

"Yeah, so would I." Mika understood Ace had a point. She just wanted him to get out the streets before they claimed him also. But she knew Ace would be a street nigga until the death of him.

"Let's just keep our heads up for lil bro," Ace encouraged.

Mika's iPhone began to ring. Looking at its display, she saw the caller was their mom, Gale, calling from federal prison. Mika picked up the phone and accepted the collect call. "Hey, Ma!"

"Hi, baby girl. Hope you and your brother is feeling better," Gale said.

"We're trying to."

"It's good to hear your voice. I just wish I could talk to your brother too."

"Here he is." Mika practically forced Ace to take the phone, feeling he needed to talk with their mom now more than ever.

Ace reluctantly spoke into the phone. "Sup, Ma?"

"Hey, son!" Gale was ecstatic. It was the first time she had heard his voice in a while. "Listen, I'm sorry about what happened to Glen. I know it's hard on you and your sister. It pains me that I'm not able to be there for y'all in this hard time. But I'll be home soon."

"Look, Ma, don't feel too bad. It's not like you haven't been tryin' to reach out to me and lil bro, we were just too damn stubborn to care. But I want us to talk more now, 'cause I'ont know when my life may come to an end in these streets," Ace replied in sincerity. He and his moms weren't on the best of terms, but he wanted that to change.

"Ace, don't talk like that," Gale responded, finding his reply hard to take.

"Just look at what happened to Glen. His life was stolen young. And before I let a nigga take me out, I'ma slide on whoever did that shit to lil bro and make sure they ain't able to do shit to Mika," he growled.

Gale could hear in his voice he was dead serious. "I understand what you're saying, son. But it's not what you do, it's how you do it. I already lost Glen, and I don't want to lose you too. Plus, your sister needs you in her life as much as I do."

"I feel you, Ma."

"I know I was caught up in the game too much to be there for y'all like a mother should be, but I did those things to take care of y'all. And this is just part of the same game you're playing. So, just be willing to respect the game as it is," she schooled him.

"Fa sho. Just know from now on I'm here for you."

"Good. I love you, son."

Ace thought about it for a moment. "Luh you too, Ma."

After receiving the phone back, Mika talked with Gale a few more minutes before the collect call ended. She shifted towards Ace and said, "Mama wants us to keep our heads up. It was good that you talked with her 'cause she really miss you and Glen. I get why y'all was mad at her for not being here for us, but she has always loved us. And now she loves us even more after losing Glen."

"Talkin' with her was good for me too. And from now on, I'ma be here for her," he assured. "I just hate it took for us to

10

lose Gee for me and her to reconcile. Speakin' of Gee, how 'bout we get back to the vigil." Ace took a moment in the car while Mika exited and headed back to the vigil with the others. He grabbed a small sack of Percocet tablets and washed one down. The pills seemed to ease the pain of losing his brother.

Chedda tapped on the passenger window and gestured for Ace to come and join the vigil. Chedda and some others from the hood were taking photos on their cellphones, and Ace pulled Mika in a few. Next, Ace and only his boys took a couple more photos, all wearing T-shirts with pictures of Glen on them. They were representin' for Gee.

It had grown dark outside, and Mika passed out candles to everyone who wanted one. She had the DJ stop the music, and then grabbed the microphone. She said some loving words about Gee before passing the mic to Reverend Johnson.

"Brothers, sisters, and children," Rev started his sermon. "I want to announce my condolences. We're all gathered here in such grief. This is a sad moment, not only because we're here with one emotion, but also because we now have loss another fine young man in Glen." Rev eyed the crowd. Majority of them were youngsters. "This is a message from the Lord to our young future. See, I believe a lot of us old heads forget the children are our future. I remember growing up during a time when things were old-school, and parents believed that it takes a village to raise a child. Nowadays, kids are brought up on what's seen on television, what's viral online and what's heard from rap lyrics. So, our community is filled with violence because the younger generation is chasing one motive. Get rich or die trying.

"You see, young brothers and sisters, we're lost in a delusional state of mind. Living in a world that has also stripped many of us of our cultural heritage and identity. This obviously has left a gaping hole in the minds of many of us.

Now, it appears the gaping hole has been filled with the notion that being rich and famous above all else, automatically makes us acceptable. Therefore, somehow, we must get rich or die trying. Brothers and sisters, I'm here to tell you all that if you follow God's plan, you'll live in a life of luxury without selling drugs, prostituting, robbing, and killing. The Lord will lead you."

Claps and applause came from the crowd. "Amen! Preach, Reverend!" an elder woman shouted from within the large crowd of faces. The Reverend hoped his sermon would save someone's life today.

Rev went on. "Now, let us please have a moment of silence for our dearly departed, Glen."

Before the moment of silence took place, Mika asked everyone to light their candles, and she lit the ones surrounding the shrine. Everyone bowed their heads in silence with thoughts of Gee. After the candlelight ceremony, Ace found Paris then gave her the keys to his car and told her to take their son home. He walked them to the Acura and let Paris know he would be home later. Once his girl and son were gone, then Ace approached all of his boys, who were standing near Gee's shrine.

"I hate that we gotta be here like this for Gee, but good lookin' for the love," Ace told his boys.

"Fuck happened tonight, Ace?" Chedda wanted to know the details.

"Like I told you, while I was at Mika's crib, me and Gee was on the front porch talkin', when a silver sedan spun the block on us with a shooter hangin' out the window bustin'."

"You sure you didn't see who the mu'fucka was doin' the bustin'?"

"Naw, I didn't, 'cause me and Gee was too busy bustin' back. But before all that shit went down, I did happen to see

12

that same car parked outside the liquor store, it was a Benz. I just couldn't see who the fuck was inside 'cause the windows were tinted. Right then I shoulda known some shit was wrong." Ace realized whoever was in the sedan that night had tailed him, looking for a chance to catch him when he least expected it.

"Don't even blame yourself for this shit 'cause it ain't your fault," Chedda consoled.

"But those bitch-ass niggas got Gee. They got my lil brotha!" Ace breathed furiously. "He went out bustin'. Gee went out like a savage."

"Damn, Ace. I can't even imagine how you feelin' after seein' Gee die like that and shit," Bookie uttered.

Ace fought back tears as he thought about his lil brother being dead. "That shit feels different seein' him dyin'."

"On Gee, we gon' smoke whoever did this shit. First, we gotta find out who the hell it was," Poppa said.

"Any word on who did it?" Sly asked no one in particular.

Since the night of the shooting, Ace n'em had been trying to figure out who could've popped Gee. "No word yet. But as soon as I get any, then we gonna slide on whoever the niggas is," Ace told them. He realized it could have been Stone who sent the shooters, after their fight during the block party. Or, it could have been some of Skinny's niggas out for retaliation after he got murked. But there were also others that could have been behind the hit. Yet, he couldn't point his trigger finger at who it was for sure.

"Maybe it was that nigga, Stone. He been wantin' beef with us," Bookie suggested.

"Or it could be some of Skinny niggas out for retaliation after he got murked," Poppa added.

"Y'all right, maybe it could be Stone or Skinny's niggas. But we can't just slide on them until we know fa sho. All due respect, I wanna whack whoever did this shit to my lil brotha, more than any of y'all. And I won't be satisfied 'til they not breathin'," Ace asserted.

Chedda felt compelled to speak up. "Gee was like my lil brotha too, Ace, so I ain't lettin' niggas get away with killin' him like that. We in this shit together." He knew Ace would need him now more than ever. "Listen dawg, you gotta make sure you stay on your feet in these streets, 'cause niggas tryin' to catch you slippin'. Can't let them get you out the way."

"Chedda, I'ma be out here in these streets till I find the niggas who got my lil brotha. Them niggas shoulda killed me too," Ace warned.

"You already know I'm down for whatever, my nigga." Chedda understood Ace had the mentality to kill or get killed looking for some get back. "On Gee, we gon' smoke whoever did this shit."

Ace looked to his boys. "Niggas know we gon' slide for Gee. 'Til then, we gon' run it up and we gon' stay poled up."

"No cap, any nigga can get it," Chedda added, and all of the others agreed.

"Look, I'ma get home to my bitch and son," Ace told them. "Chedda, gimme a ride to the crib."

Ace and Chedda shook up with the rest of the gang before heading for the Audi. As Chedda pulled off down the street, Ace's phone began to ring. He looked at the display and saw it was Kiki, then answered.

"Whassup, Ki."

"I was just thinking about you. You okay?" Kiki asked out of concern.

"Yeah, I'm good. But niggas better know we ain't gon' play 'bout Gee."

"Well, I think you should know Stone posted a live video on his *Facebook*, talking shit."

"Talkin' shit about' what?"

"Just stop by my ma's house and I'll let you see the video yourself."

"A'ight. I'll be there." After Ace ended the call with Kiki, he looked to Chedda.

"What it do, my boy?" Chedda wanted to know.

"That was Kiki. She told me the nigga Stone posted a video talkin' shit, and she want me to see the shit myself."

"Fuck is his bitch-ass talkin' 'bout?"

"I'ont know. But let's go and find out."

"Where she at?"

"Her ma's crib."

"A'ight, we on our way."

Once they arrived at the location, Chedda parked the Audi near the curb. Ace stepped out of the car, toting his Glock in the front pocket of his Balmain jeans, with its extended clip protruding. Chedda remained sitting inside the car while Ace approached Kiki, who was seated on the porch steps beside a pregnant Red and another bitch.

"Hey, Ace," Kiki greeted him. "Look, I'm sorry about Glen. You know how much I loved your brother."

"Yeah, I know. And lil bro loved you too, Kiki. I hate that niggas took him from us, and I'ma smoke whoever did it," Ace promised.

"Then you need to see this video of Stone talking about how you know what it is and shit."

"Fuck that nigga, and any nigga ridin' with him!" Ace snapped. "Now, what you got for me to see?" He was eager to see the video. Kiki handed him her iPhone, and he watched the video.

Sitting inside his red Chrysler 300C, Stone was smoking on a blunt while talking shit into the camera. "That bitch-nigga

Ace thought shit was sweet, so I had my shooter catch his ass slippin'. Now him and his niggas know what it is."

Stone's shooter, Duke, brandished a .223 assault rifle on camera and began bragging in the background. "Yeah, I missed Ace bitch-ass. But I smoked Gee like a blunt!"

The video pissed off Ace. Having seen enough, he handed Kiki back her phone and stated, "Don't trip. I'ma pull up on them bitch-ass niggas ASAP."

After giving Kiki a hug, Ace turned and hopped back into the passenger's seat of the Audi. As Chedda pulled off down the block, Ace filled him in on what was up. It was well-known that Duke was one of Stone's real shooters. Now it was no doubt Stone was behind the hit, and Ace most definitely wouldn't let him get away with it. He wasn't surprised Stone was the one who had sent shooters at him. And since Gee was the one murdered instead of himself, it made Ace thirsty for vengeance.

"That nigga Stone gon' get his. And Duke too," Chedda stated while pushing the whip through traffic.

"On Gee, we gon' kill them bitch-ass niggas," Ace vowed.

Chapter 2

It had been a month since Gee's murder, and Ace n'em was beefin' heavily with Stone and his gang. So much so, several bodies had been dropping on either side. However, Ace hadn't been able to run across the nigga Stone thus far. As of late, Stone couldn't be found dead around the hood, word was he moved far out to some ducked off location. On the other hand, Ace n'em had put the hood on lock., They provided it with guns and flooded it with yae. Though they were in beef, there was still money to be made.

Ace, along with Chedda, was on the way to meet up with the plug, Shane. They had flipped their last load and was looking forward to Shane giving them seven bricks on consignment as planned. Although Ace felt they could move even more work, he also got the feeling Chedda was content with what they were working with. But the game was about gettin' their money and weight up.

"Chedda, we been fuckin' with ya boy, Shane, for a lil while now. Don't you think he should front us more weight? Plus, we always come with our money correct," Ace said from the passenger seat of the Audi.

"I hear you, my nigga. But I just don't want us to get too far into debt with Shane. 'Cause soon, I plan to fall back from this street shit and go legit," Chedda replied as he pushed the Audi through traffic.

"Well, I'ma hold down the streets while you take care of the legit shit. Besides, after what happened with Gee, ain't no way in hell I'm gonna let niggas breathe in these streets."

"Even though we have beef, there's still money to be made. Only problem is, gettin' money and beefin' don't mix so well. As long as the bodies keep droppin', then twelve will

17

continue to sweat the hood, which makes it difficult for us to move product."

"I know. So, we need to catch Stone in order to end so much of the beef in the hood and prevent twelve from slowin' up the money. And even with Lucas tryin' to jam me up, I won't stop tryin' to smoke Stone's bitch-ass."

The beef was so deadly, the crooked cop Lucas and his partner in crime, Bradshaw, made it a point to arrest as many from the hood as they could., Even if they had to plant drugs and guns on their culprits. But Lucas had it out for Ace more than anyone. So much so, Lucas had been harassing people from around the hood, including Mika, to snitch on Ace for the murders that were taking place in the area. Although, no one would cooperate. After that night Ace had shot at him, Lucas was hellbent on putting him in prison for life. But Ace wasn't willing to go back to prison no matter what, he would rather hold court in the streets.

"My nigga, I know you wanna smoke Stone, and so do I. But what about Phat? He's still liable to become a problem," Chedda deliberated.

"Yeah, whenever I catch Stone then I'ma shoot his fuckin' face off," Ace told him. "As for Phat, I'ont trust him like I did Baller. I find it suspect that Phat ducked that indictment any fuckin' way. But for now, I'ma play his ass close."

Chedda braked at a stoplight. "Ace, I'ont want neither of us to end up gettin' indicted. Or worse."

"We both know that's the type of shit that comes with the street life."

"And that's why we need to go legit with this strip joint and shit."

"But it don't mean we have to stop trappin'. We can use the club and shit to our advantage," Ace suggested. Not only was he and Chedda flippin' weight, the two had invested in a strip club venture together. It was their way to go legit and launder dirty money.

"Speakin' of, I'm lookin' at a few different spots that would be best for us to open the club. It ain't official as of yet, although I got the lawyer handlin' all of the legal work in order to make our business legitimate. And did you find any bad bitches for us to potentially hire at the club?"

"Not yet. But I did talk with my lil bitch, Savvy, about it. And she's gonna help us find some baddies."

"A'ight. Just let me know when she find some girls. Until then, we gonna get shit with the club together." Chedda pulled off with traffic once the light flipped green.

Shortly thereafter, Ace and Chedda arrived at Shane's auto detailing shop. Once Chedda parked the Audi out front, he then stepped out, toting a backpack filled with cash from the previous flip. And Ace made sure his .45 Glock was ready for action, then he stuffed it in the front pocket of his Off-White jeans, its thirty-two-shot stick protruding, before he followed suit. As much as Chedda trusted Shane, Ace just wasn't willing to take any chances with no muthafucka when so much cash and drugs was on the line. The deal went accordingly, all the cash Ace and Chedda had brought along was exchanged for the seven birds Shane had offered up as a front.

Once the deal was done, Ace and Chedda jumped back in traffic. They were on their way to the trap spot in the hood, where they would prepare the work for distribution. Chedda drove real smooth on the expressway because he didn't want to give twelve any reason to attempt pulling them over while they were ridin' dirty. There were a couple times Ace had to tell his ass to watch the road when he noticed Chedda looked at a text on his iPhone. When they made it to the hood, Chedda pulled to the curb in front of their trap spot.

Ace grabbed the backpack now stuffed with kilos and stepped out the Audi, and Chedda followed. Poppa and Bookie were posted out on the block in the company of some bitches. They were Ace's two favorite lil homies, since they had been so close to Gee. And both of them were down for whatever.

"What's good, big bros?" Bookie greeted them.

"Nothin' much," Chedda said.

"Y'all niggas best be strapped while y'all posted out here," Ace told them, knowing they were in serious beef.

Poppa raised his shirt just enough to show the butt of his glizzy with a thirty-shot stick on it, and replied, "You know I keep it on me. And Bookie got the street-sweeper ducked off in the cut."

"A'ight. Now check this bitch out," Ace said as he pulled out the .45 Glock fitted with an extended clip and a converter switch. "Had to upgrade my firepower with all the beef and shit."

"Damn, big bro, I see you ready to chop a nigga in half!" Bookie admired the choppa-like handgun.

Ace replaced the pipe in his pocket. While Ace n'em were posted on the block, his iPhone rang, and he peeped the call was from a nigga named Roach from around the hood. Ace n'em didn't really know the nigga, Roach normally just copped weed from Ace, for the most part.

"Whassup?" Ace answered.

"What's good, Ace? I wanna holla at you real quick," Roach said.

"A'ight."

"Look, I got a gun for sale."

"Lemme buy it. Pull up on the block."

"Cool. I'm right around the corner."

Ace ended the call with every intention to come up on another weapon. With all the beef he had with Stone, Ace needed as much artillery as he could get his hands on.

"Who dat?" Chedda asked.

"Roach. Nigga say he got a pole for sale. We need that," Ace told him.

"Fa sho."

Soon thereafter, a white Chevy Caprice turned onto the block then pulled over to the curb. Roach stepped out and then approached Ace, who was flanked by his niggas.

"Let's see the pole real quick," Ace suggested.

Roach pulled the MAC-10 off his waist, then took the bullets out before handing it over to Ace for examination. Suddenly, Ace upped his .45 on Roach and aimed at his head.

"Damn!" Roach cried out.

"Nigga, get the fuck on," Ace insisted.

"It's like that?"

"If I'ont know you, I'ma hoe you. Suck it up, 'cause I'll smoke you. Now, act like you want some beef and I'll show you!" Ace asserted.

"Say no more."

Roach hurried back to his car as Ace stuffed both poles on his waist. Once Roach stepped into his Chevy, Ace n'em watched as Roach smashed off down the street.

"Dawg, your ass is a fool with it!" Bookie laughed.

"On Gee, if niggas ain't with the gang, then it's open season," Ace stated.

"Straight like that," Poppa seconded.

"That nigga Roach a sweet thang any fuckin' way," Chedda said, shaking his head.

Ace handed the MAC to Poppa, and said, "Put that with the rest of the burners."

Chedda received a text and read it. "Check it out, take the work and go and get it together. I gotta get home and see what the fuck my BM keeps textin' me about. I'll be back later."

"Damn, my boy. BM stay on your ass," Ace half-joked.

Chedda chuckled. "Nigga, stop actin' like your BM don't be on your ass too."

"Paris know I ain't havin' that shit, so she don't say nothin' while I'm out here in these streets chasin' a bag."

"Yeah, right. Bet her ass have somethin' to say if she finds out you fuckin' off on her," Chedda jabbed.

"As long as I'm takin' care of her and my son, then she can't say shit. Feel me. And Chedda, don't sit here actin' like you don't be fuckin' off too."

Chedda shook his damn head and snorted. "The difference between me and you is, I'ont have feelings for another bitch."

"Whatever, nigga." Ace had to admit his boy had a point. "Go ahead. I'll take care of this shit."

After he shook up with the gang, Chedda returned to his whip. He honked the horn at the gang as he pulled down the block on his way.

"Look, I need y'all to come with me real quick. Where's Sly at?" Ace said.

"In the spot. Why, whassup?" Poppa asked.

"Just come with me, lil bro."

Ace led the way inside the trap spot with Poppa and Bookie in tow. Soon as they entered, Gee's pitbull, Beast-Mode, excitedly jumped all over Ace. Sly was in the front room seated on the couch, while counting up some cash on the coffee table. Ace unzipped the backpack then dumped the bricks atop the coffee table for them to get a look at.

"We need to cut these keys and at least stretch six ounces outta each one of 'em," Ace said, more-so to Sly.

"Say no more. I can make that happen," Sly assured.

"Then once that's done, we'll bag up three bricks in twenty- and fifty-pieces. And the rest we'll sell in eight-balls and zips. The first two-hundred-and-fifty-bands will be for re-up, and the rest will be all profit," Ace laid out.

Of them all, Sly knew how to cut dope the best, since he used to smoke the shit before getting himself all cleaned up. He hadn't always used drugs. At first, he was the drug dealer, so Sly understood the game from both sides. And now he was the one Ace n'em had overseeing most of their trap spots.

Ace n'em had offered Sly a seat at the table ever since he earned it after getting off the pipe. Ace liked to make sure all of his niggas were eatin'. But if any of them decided to bite the hand that fed them, then Ace would deal with them drastically. Thus far, that wasn't an issue at the table, because Ace kept his niggas well fed. However, he was conscious there was always potential for greed.

Martell "Troublesome" Bolden

Chapter 3

It was early in the a.m. when Ace pulled up outside Savvy's crib and parked near the curb. Noticing her Chrysler Sebring parked in the driveway was a sign that Savvy had to be home. He stepped out the Acura and then made his way to the front door, using his key to allow himself inside.

The house was quiet. *Savvy must still be asleep, since her ass didn't even reply to the text I sent her while on the way,* Ace thought. He knew after long nights at the club, she normally slept in during mornings. Making his way into the bedroom, Ace found Savvy in bed asleep under the covers with her bestie, Nina, beside her. He had thought about having a threesome with Savvy and Nina before, but right now he was there to collect some product from his stash so he could go and catch some plays for the day.

Not bothering to awake either of the girls, Ace went over to the closet where his stash was beneath the floorboard. He put a bundle of cash with the rest and then grabbed a half brick of yae and a pound of loud from the stash. *Damn, I'ma need to cop more weed from Abdul soon enough,* he contemplated. Once Ace turned for the door, he noticed that Nina had stirred awake, she yawned as she stretched.

"Hey, Ace. What you doing here so damn early?" Nina asked and sat up in bed.

Ace showed her the product, and replied, "Had to grab this shit real quick."

"Lemme get a blunt of that gas."

"A'ight. But you gotta sack up some of it for me," he bargained.

"That's cool," she agreed. "Just gimme a sec to take a pee and then clean myself up."

Once Nina slipped from beneath the comforter and out of bed, Ace couldn't help but admire her looking so damn good while wearing only a set of red lingerie. Her skin was sandy brown with tatts and her body was curvaceous. She was a bad-ass Latina bitch. As she waltzed to the adjacent bathroom, Nina swayed her plump ass to give Ace a mini show and to no surprise, he was checking out her ass when she peeped back over her shoulder at him before entering the bathroom. Ace glanced over and saw Savvy was still asleep, then he turned and made his way into the front room.

While Ace was busy bagging up eight-balls of the yae, he was seated on the couch with the half-brick and pound of weed set out atop the coffee table. Along with a digital scale and box of sandwich bags, there were his two iPhones and his .45 Glock. Ace was weighing up on the scale when Nina came into the front room, now wearing a Nike jogger suit and her long hair was pulled back into a messy ponytail. He scooted over on the couch as she took a seat beside him.

"That shit smell loud," Nina commented, referring to the strong aroma of the weed.

"'Cause it's real loud pack, not that regular shit niggas be movin'," Ace said. "Now, all you gotta do is—"

"Boy, I got this," Nina assured, cutting him short. "My ex-nigga used to have me do this shit for his ass all the time." She began bagging up seven-gram sacks of the weed.

"Say less."

Ace continued on bagging up the yae while Nina sacked up the loud. Half an hour later, they had more than enough product ready for distribution. He put the yae and loud in two separate Ziploc bags. Then he bagged the rest of the dope in ounces and left the rest of the weed out on the table to be smoked up.

Rich $avage 2

Once Ace's iPhone rang, he answered, it was a buyer. After ending the call, he stood and said, "I gotta go and catch a play." He grabbed the Ziploc bags and stuffed them inside his hoodie pocket, then positioned the Glock on his waist.

"Take me to pick up some breakfast for me and Savvy," Nina requested.

"Why don't you just order *DoorDash*?"

"Boy, I'ont want some stranger bringing me food. Lemme grab my purse real quick." She started for the bedroom.

"You don't need no purse. I'll take care of it. C'mon."

Ace headed out the house with Nina in tow. They stepped into the Acura and Ace pulled off down the street. He stopped at the gas station, where he sent Nina inside to purchase some petrol and a box of blunts. While he stood outside pumping the gas into the tank, Nina sat in the car rolling up a blunt of loud. His iPhone rang a few times and each time he answered, it was someone calling for a buy, so he needed to get the money. When the gas was done pumping, Ace stepped back into the car and Nina was smoking on the blunt. Once his line rang again, he tossed it in Nina's lap then started the car.

"Shorty, answer the line and just tell me where to pull up," Ace instructed her as he pulled out into traffic.

"I got you."

While Nina answered the line whenever it rang, she directed Ace where to go. Before he knew it, an hour had passed, and he sold a portion of the yae and half of the loud. The whole while Ace was riding and catchin' plays, he and Nina were holding conversation. Now he was on his way to drop her off.

"Where you wanna go to pick up somethin' to eat?" Ace asked.

"I texted Sav and asked her what she wants for breakfast, but she hasn't replied. So just go to IHOP," Nina answered.

"Her ass probably still asleep after workin' at the club so late. She always at that damn club, but soon she won't have to worry about that."

"Savvy told me you're about to open your own club, and you need some bad bitches to work there. I'ont have a problem with poppin' this pussy for you." She eyed him.

Ace braked at a stoplight. "A nigga gonna definitely need you workin' at the club. Just give it some time."

Once they arrived at IHOP, Ace parked in the lot. He remained in the car, while Nina went inside to pick up her order she had made via phone along the way.

While awaiting Nina to return, Ace lit up a half-smoked blunt. When his iPhone rang, he looked down at it in the cupholder and saw the call was from Phat.

"What it do, my boy?" Ace answered.

"Tryin' to get some money," Phat replied.

"You and me both."

"No doubt. Check it out, I wanna talk business with you. Can you pull up on me at Queen's spot later tonight?"

"Fa sho." Ace hit the blunt. He noticed Nina exiting the restaurant.

"I'ma catch up with you then. And Sonny Boy will be there also," Phat mentioned.

"That's all good," Ace told him as Nina entered the passenger seat. "My nigga, I'll just meet up with y'all at Queen's spot sometime tonight." He wrapped up the call, wondering what the fuck Phat wanted to talk with him about. Low key, Ace didn't fuck with Phat much after his suspicions about him when it came to the indictment on Baller. But for now, Ace was keeping Phat close until it was time to cut him off like karate.

Once Nina returned to the car then Ace jumped back into traffic. While he pushed the whip, he bobbed his head and rapped along with Moneybagg Yo's "Another One." Nina found herself eyeing him, she was used to fuckin' with street niggas like Ace and frankly, he was her type.

"Ace, I wanna fuck you," Nina told him, then puffed the blunt.

Ace glanced over at her and replied, "That's somethin' you gotta take up with Savvy."

"Good to know you care about my bitch feelings."

"She a real bitch, and I respect that. Besides, I thought you fuck with Phat?"

Nina smacked her sexy lips. "If you think I let Phat fuck me, then you're wrong. I mean, he's cool and all, but his fat ass ain't my type."

"It is what it is," Ace chuckled.

Making it to their destination, Ace pulled to the curb. Nina grabbed the bag of food and then stepped out of the car. He admired her plump ass briefly as she made her way towards the house before he drove away. Admittedly, he thought the bitch was bad, but he wouldn't make a move on her because she was Savvy's bestie.

Pushing the Acura eastbound on Center Street, Ace was headed to the hood. Once Ace made it there, he stopped at the liquor store. Before stepping out the car, Ace stuffed the Glock in the front pocket of his Amiri jeans. Ace went to the beverages inside the L-store and grabbed himself a bottle of Fiji water then made his way to the front counter, where Abdul stood behind the cash register. Ace waited for the only other customer to purchase her items and then leave out.

"What's good, Abdul?" Ace greeted as he lay five bucks on the counter to purchase the bottled water.

"I'm alright, buddy. Would that be all?" Abdul said.

"Actually, I need five pillows of weed."

Abdul smirked. "Lucky for you, I just got a load of some cookie weed."

"Sounds good. I'll take it."

"Just come back at closing time, and we'll talk then," Abdul told him.

Ace headed outside with the bottled water in hand. While standing in front of the L-store, Ace pulled out his iPhone, then logged into *Facebook* to see what was going on social media. He scrolled down his news feed, and of all the things, what caught his eye was the pictures Star had posted of her, Stone, and their daughter. He saw they were at Six Flags by the background. Ace scoffed and thought, *no wonder why I haven't caught that bitch-ass nigga, 'cause his ass outta town.* Now Ace knew he needed to be patient to find Stone and would keep that in mind.

Ace was finna make a post himself but yielded when one of the lil homies approached him, looking to cop a bag of weed. He served lil homie, then Ace entered the Acura and headed on his way to make serves.

***

Later that night, Queen's gamble spot was poppin', as usual. There was always big money either being won or loss, and tonight was no different. Ace was there with Phat and Sonny Boy. Not to mention, Nice and Troy were present. Earlier, Phat had called Ace and Sonny to show up at the gamble spot, where they would talk some business. The trio were in a secluded corner talking amongst themselves, while Nice and Troy were in close proximity on security.

"Since shit has been goin' so well between us, I'ma hit you with four bricks durin' my next load," Phat told Sonny.

"And what are you expectin' in return?" Sonny inquired.

"A hunnit G's."

"Fair exchange ain't a robbery," Sonny said in agreement. Phat turned to Ace. "Check it out, I'll be goin' on another trip to Chiraq soon, and I want you to roll with me again to pick up a load. It'll pay you ten G's."

"That's a bet," Ace agreed. "Just lemme know when we rollin' out."

"A'ight. And speakin' of bets, let's go shoot some dice." Phat turned for the crowd of crap shooters, and Ace and Sonny Boy trailed him.

They were all engaged in the dice game, and the stakes was high. Ace placed a side bet for a band on Sonny Boy to hit his point on the dice. Sonny shook up the dice, then rolled them over the table a few times, until he eventually hit his point and won all bets against him. Thus far, Ace had hit the gamble for some over six G's. Sonny Boy made conservative bets. However, Phat was a gambleholic. He waged thousands of dollars, but his money was long, so it wasn't shit to him.

After Sonny Boy finally rolled craps on the dice, he stepped back and counted up the monies he had won. While Phat continued placing more bets on the dice game, Ace took a moment away from the gamble to rap with Sonny.

"Let's go and roll up a blunt," Ace suggested.

"I'm with that," Sonny seconded while calculating his winnings.

The two stepped into the crowd of dice shooters and let Phat know they were about to bounce. Phat decided to remain in the gamble spot after losing big, so he could try and win his damn money back. Ace and Sonny Boy headed outside and into the night that was lit up by only the dim streetlights. Ace grabbed his stick out of his car, just in case of any beef. Then he and Sonny Boy occupied Sonny's silver Audi SUV that was parked across the street from the gamble spot. While they were smoking on a blunt of the loud pack Ace had on deck, Lil Durk's track "Street Prayer" played at a lowered volume in the background.

"Damn, homeboy, this shit smokin'!" Sonny exclaimed. The thick weed smoke caused him to cough.

"I get that shit from my weed connect for the low," Ace told him. He remembered that he needed to go and see Abdul for a re-up.

After puffing the blunt once more, Sonny passed it. "I'ma need to cop a few zips of that smoke, no cap."

"I keep it on deck. Just hit me up whenever." Ace hit the blunt. "I see shit is really pickin' up with you and Phat," he mentioned.

"Ever since I been fuckin' with him, I done got my money and weight up," Sonny Boy told him. "Plus, my brotha comin' home soon, and I wanna be able to show him some love. So, this next load from Phat would help with that."

"Just be your own boss, and don't let Phat or no nigga prevent that," Ace offered him words of advice.

"I hear you, my nigga."

Ace puffed the blunt once more then passed it back to Sonny, and said, "You can enjoy that. Just gimme a call whenever you wanna cop some. I gotta go take care of shit."

After they parted, Ace was on his way to pull up on Abdul for a re-up. He knew that keeping product on deck is how money piled up.

Chapter 4

Ace pulled up in front of Mika's crib and parked the Acura. For a moment he and his son remained sitting in the car under the air-conditioning. It was crawling into full-fledged summer, and the warming weather was sure to let it be known. Niggas had run it up all winter, just so they could pull out when the summertime hit, including Ace. But he knew Milwaukee's summers were considered killing season, so much so, the natives of the city had dubbed it Killwaukee.

After he had picked up Adonis from daycare, Ace was finna drop his son off at Mika's crib. He had to catch some plays and didn't want to have Adonis with him while doing so with all the beef in play. Plus, he knew Paris preferred for him to either be at home with Adonis or leave him with Mika, in order to keep their son out of harm's way. As soon as Ace was done handling his business he would be back for his son.

Ace grabbed up Adonis then stepped out into the heat and made his way inside the house. Upon entering the front room, Ace found Mika seated on the couch beside Kiki. They were packing up boxes and preparing for Mika's move out to Green Bay. So far, about a quarter of her things were packed up and ready to be moved. And soon she would be moving out of the hood.

"Go and play with Breon," Ace told Adonis as he planted him on the floor. Adonis took off towards his big cousin's bedroom.

"Hey, bro," Mika greeted as she taped a box closed.

"What's good, sis. And whaddup with you, Kiki?" he greeted them.

"I'm okay. Just helping out big sis," Kiki replied.

"I see you really packin' your shit up, Mika," he pointed out.

"Yep. Part of me don't wanna move. But I just need to go somewhere where it'll be safer living," Mika said.

"Mika, you ain't wrong. Just remember I'll always be a phone call away."

"I know, bro."

"Look, I'ma be back to pick up my son in a lil while. I gotta go and chase a bag real quick," Ace let her know.

Mika peered at him and said, "Ace, don't think I'ma be watching his bad ass for free. Gimme some money, nigga."

"Damn, sis, it's like that?" Ace reached into the pocket of his Nike jogger pants and pulled out a sloppy bundle of cash. He gave Mika two hundred bucks before putting the money away. "I'll be back later."

Kiki stood. "Big bro, gimme a ride home. Mika, I'll call you later, girl."

Ace left out with Kiki trailing him. While Kiki sat in the passenger seat, Ace took a moment to visit Gee's shrine. Kiki knew Ace blamed himself for what happened to Gee. It wasn't a day that went by when Ace didn't miss his lil brotha. And he still yearned to make sure Stone stopped breathing.

As Reverend Johnson parked his Cadillac in front of his home, he noticed Ace. Rev knew Ace was still hurt behind the loss of Glen, he just didn't want Ace to get himself killed, being so determined to seek vengeance. Stepping out of his car, Rev made his way over to Ace and stood beside him.

"How do you feel, son?" Rev inquired.

"I'm a'ight," Ace answered neutrally.

"No, son. How do you really feel? I can see all over your face that losing your brother is still very much so hard on you. But remember it's all in God's plan."

Ace looked to Rev and remarked, "All due respect, God seems to have a fucked-up plan for me then. I'ont understand why He would put me through so much."

"God gives his toughest battles to his strongest soldiers, son." Rev placed a hand on Ace's shoulder. "And if there's anything I know about you, it's that you're stronger than most. But don't you ever mistake guns and money as your strengths."

"I feel you, Rev. Look, I gotta go." Ace turned for his whip.

"You be safe, son. And pull up your britches," Rev called out behind him.

Ace pulled up his sagging jogging pants as he stepped into the driver's side of his Acura. He honked the horn at Reverend Johnson as he pulled away from the curb. Ace rode with his pole in his lap. Making it around the corner, he yielded the whip in the middle of the street in front of Kiki's place. She was finna step out, but then stopped.

"Hold up, Ace. You know I still have your lil brotha car, money, phone and guns, right?" Kiki mentioned.

"Yeah. Why, you want me to take it all?" he asked.

"Naw, I'ma need it. That's if you'll hit me with some work to move, and then I'll just cop my re-up from you."

Ace smirked. "Kiki, do you even know how to fuck with work?"

"Yeah, dude. Gee had taught me how to cook it, bag it, and sell it. I used to be out all night trappin' and shit with his ass. Don't worry about it, I know what I'm doing, big bro. Plus, I got Gee's guns, and he taught me how to use them too."

Ace leaned back in his seat and studied her for a moment. "A'ight, lil sis. I got you. I'll pull up on you later with somethin'."

"Cool. See you later, big bro." Kiki stepped out of the car and then Ace drove off.

After Neesha was killed by the nigga Skinny, due to servin' weed for Ace, he was hesitant to have Kiki serve dope for him. But Ace could see Kiki had it in her to be a pretty savage, and he didn't doubt she could hold her own. Besides, most wouldn't dare try to rob or finesse her, after suspecting Ace had smoked Skinny for that same shit.

When he pulled up and parked in front of the trap spot, like usual, Poppa and Bookie were posted up with some other niggas from the hood, reminding Ace of his days of being posted on the block with his pole cocked. As the two approached the car, Ace peeped that Poppa seemed to be walking with a limp. He pressed a button and automatically unlocked the doors, then Bookie slid into the front seat and Poppa took up the back with his wounded leg lying across the seat.

"Fuck happened to your ass?" Ace questioned Poppa, looking back at him, while Bookie snickered.

"Man, last night I fucked around and popped myself in the thigh," Poppa admitted ruefully.

Bookie burst out laughing. "Told this stupid-ass nigga to stop always playin' with his gun."

"Shut the fuck up, Bookie. Always got some shit to say. Opps know I'm all about gunplay!" Poppa remarked.

"Both of you niggas need to be easy," Ace piped in. "Ride with me real quick."

While in traffic, Ace texted his pill man, Mane, to meet with him at the gas station in the hood. He needed to get his mind right with a Percocet tablet. Once Ace made it to the location, he pulled the Acura to a gas pump. He pocketed the glizzy, stepped out the whip and made his way into the station. Bookie waisted his Glock and then got out to pump the gas, while Poppa remained seated in the car with the MAC-10 in his lap, watching out for any opps. And as Ace was at the counter paying for some gas and a bottle of Fiji water, he peeped Mane's silver Lexus pull into the lot and park near the entrance. Making his way outside, Ace then approached the passenger side of the Lex and entered. He couldn't help but notice the diamonds around Mane's neck and the stick across his lap.

"What it do, fool?" Mane greeted.

"Shit. Tryin' to get lit," Ace said. "What you taxin' for two Percs?"

"Just gimme fifty bucks."

Ace paid him and in return he received two Percocet-20 tablets. "Check it out, I got work and smoke for the low if you need that shit."

"I'll hit you up if I need to cop some." Mane's line rang and he looked at its display briefly then swiped "Ignore." It began to immediately ring again. "I gotta go and chase a check. Holla at me."

Ace stepped out of the Lexus, and then Mane pulled off on his way. Once Ace returned to the Acura, he popped one of the pills and washed it down with a drink from the bottled water. He knew not to give Bookie and Poppa no pills when they had their guns, because lil dawg n'em too dangerous. He started the whip, then jumped back into traffic, bobbing his head to Lil Durk's tune "TherlBread."

After shooting to catch some plays, Ace dipped to Savvy's crib real quick. Savvy wasn't there. He parked and then hurried inside. First, he went to the bathroom and took a piss after drinking the majority of the bottled water to keep himself hydrated. Afterwards, he headed to his stash and put away his profits with the rest, and then grabbed a brick of yae. Leaving out of the house, Ace locked it up. When he returned to the car, he sat the brick on his lap, along with his switch before pulling off. Ace had plans for the brick to make sure all of his people were eatin' in the streets.

"Listen," Ace began. He lowered the volume on the stereo just enough to talk over the music. "Kiki hollered at me about puttin' her on. I'ma go ahead and do it. But I want y'all to make sure she get her sack off, which shouldn't be hard 'cause she still has Gee's money-phone. And if she has any problems, then y'all solve that shit ASAP. I'ont want nothin' to happen to her. Feel me."

"You know she's like our sis," Bookie concurred.

"Yeah, so she got our love," Poppa input.

"Fa sho. And I'm sure Gee would wanna see y'all niggas out here eatin' in these streets, so I'ma break bread with y'all too. Those sacks y'all been flippin' is light shit, I'ma front y'all with some weight," Ace told them as he braked at a stoplight on Silverspring Street. He knew Pop and Boo were getting their money up, but he wanted them to have money to blow. Grabbing the brick, Ace handed it over to Bookie. "Make sure y'all give Kiki four-and-a-split, the rest is y'all's. Let's get it, we all can eat 'cause I'm in a good position."

Poppa rubbed his hands together and added, "I'm with that."

"That's all love, big bro," Bookie said gratefully.

Ace shifted in his seat and eyed both of his lil bros, then vented, "It be crazy 'cause the ones you love in competition. If it's like that, then just kill me, don't alley-hoop me to the opps."

"Stop it, big bro. You should know we'll never backdoor you like that," Poppa assured.

"Just feel me, pay attention, it ain't hard to listen. Niggas were my homies, now they keep their distance. Damn, that's why I wish Gee could call my phone so he could rap with me," Ace went on. The Perc tablet he popped had him reminiscing.

"Listen…on Gee, we gon' get some get-back when it comes to Stone," Bookie swore.

"And I hear the shit that Stone be sayin', it gets back to me. But niggas gotta run their mouths 'cause we run the hood. So, we gon' keep sticks on our poles, man, I love these bitches." Ace admired the .45 Glock with an extended clip in his lap. "Just remember, one snitch will take the whole gang away, and thoroughbreds make sacrifices," he stated, dropping jewels on them.

Once the light turned green, Ace pulled off with traffic and turned up the music to a modest volume. He just wanted all of them to be rich as hell, going from sleeping in trap houses to living in dream houses. Ace was determined for him and his niggas to make it from nothin' to somethin'. He wouldn't cross the ones he was loyal to, but fuck everybody else.

Martell "Troublesome" Bolden

Chapter 5

"Oooh, shit, baby! It feels sooo good!"

"You love this dick, don't you?"

"Yaaas, I love it so much!"

It was early in the morning. Ace and Paris were gettin' in a quickie, while Adonis was in the front room busy eating a bowl of Fruity Pebbles and watching cartoons. They had to find the time to fuck whenever they could.

Paris was bent over the edge of the bed, gripping the sheets, while Ace stood behind her digging her out. Her back was arched, and ass was tooted up, giving him full access to her wet-shot. He palmed her ass in both hands and dug his pipe inside of her until he was balls deep.

"Tell me, what do you mean to me?" Ace ordered as he fucked her.

Paris looked back at him over her shoulder and moaned, "I mean everything to you."

"Don't you ever forget that shit either, Paris." He pulled his dick out, turned her around and sat her on the edge of the bed. She held him at the shoulders and spread her legs, then he slid his dick in her creaminess. Ace slipped every inch of himself back and forth in the pussy. It felt so good to him as he was hitting her G-spot.

"Oh, my goodness... I'm... I'm cummin', baby!" Paris's body racked with orgasm, and she dug her manicured nails into his flesh as her warm cum juices ran down Ace's inner thighs.

Ace lay Paris back and held her legs up on his shoulders then pounded his hardness deep in her wetness. He felt a nut creeping into the tip of his dick. As Ace came, he grunted, "Damn, bae, you got a nigga nuttin'."

The couple lay beside one another in bed, catching their breath. Paris enjoyed the moments she got to spend with Ace, because with him always out on the paper chase, she saw him less than she would like to. Part of her felt his ass was also creeping on her with some bitch. But Paris tried giving him the benefit of the doubt. Maybe she was just being insecure. She rolled onto her side and eyed him through slits.

"Whassup, bae?" Ace asked, curiously.

"Why do you always ask me what do I mean to you, Ace?" Paris answered the question with a question.

Ace sat up on edge of the bed. "'Cause, I want you to know what you mean to a nigga."

"If I really mean everything to you, then it should mean there's no other bitch around." She studied him.

"Paris, let's not go there, a'ight?" Ace was annoyed. He knew he couldn't tell Paris about Savvy because it would only cause drama, so he decided to keep it to himself. "Listen..." His iPhone rang, interrupting him. Grabbing his phone off the nightstand, he saw the call was from Phat, and said, "Lemme see what dawg ass want."

Paris stood, getting out of bed. "Okay. But dude, don't let me find out your ass been out in these streets creeping and shit behind my back," she warned, before turning for the bathroom.

What her ass don't know won't hurt her, Ace mused as he answered the phone.

"Where you at? I'm about to come and scoop you up," Phat told him.

"I'm at the crib." Ace headed towards the closet to grab out a 'fit. "Where we goin'?"

"We about to go to Chiraq to take care of that business."

"Say less. Just pull up," Ace said before ending the call. He laid out a black Dior jogger suit and black Dior sneakers on the bed. Then he stepped into the bathroom on Paris, unannounced.

"Damn, boy, you rude!" Paris cried out. She was sitting on the toilet taking a tinkle.

Ace grabbed his toothbrush, and said, "I'm finna get myself together real quick, so I can bounce."

"And where are you going?" She wiped herself with tissue, then flushed it down the toilet.

"To bust a move in Chicago."

"Make sure you gimme a call if anything happens." Paris washed her hands before leaving him alone.

While Ace took care of his nine, he thought about how Chedda didn't like the idea of him still fuckin' with Phat. He understood where Chedda was coming from, especially since Ace knew eventually, Phat would become competition in the game.

***

During the trip to Chicago, the group rode in a rented black Beamer SUV. Ace and Phat took up the backseat with a duffel bag full of re-up money in between them, while Nice rode shotgun and Troy drove. The whole car was strapped, but not with any seatbelts.

By now Ace was used to taking the trip, because every time Phat had to go to the city for re-up, he brought Ace along as a hired gun. Undoubtedly, Phat trusted Nice and Troy as shooters, although having an additional one in Ace always put him at ease, with so much cash and product at stake. And Ace didn't mind acting as Phat's shooter for a fee of ten G's.

"This time around, we won't be stayin' in a telly overnight," Phat was saying. "After I meet up with the plug and pick up the load, we gon' slide back to the Mil. 'Cause I gotta get back to the money."

"Same here," Ace piped in. "Gotta make sure my money is comin' back right."

Phat shifted towards him. "You know, I respect you bein' your own boss. But you should cop weight from me, and I guarantee I'll give you the opportunity to make a lot more paper. See how I show love to Sonny Boy."

"Not unless you gon' show me the same love I used to get from the big homie, Baller." Ace studied Phat and noticed he grew tense once Baller was brought up.

"No sneak dis, but whatever you had with Baller ain't got shit to do with me. Besides, that nigga ain't out here in these streets to be a factor anymore," Phat sniped.

Ace eyed him narrowly and stated, "One thing fa sho, at least ain't no police shit on Baller's name, so his name is still good in these streets."

"Yeah, whatever." Phat snorted. He sat back in his seat. "On some other shit, what's up with the bitch Nina? Been hittin' shorty up but her ass claims she's busy."

Ace couldn't help but think back to Nina telling him Phat isn't her type. Instead, Ace told him, "Savvy and Nina stay busy workin' at the strip club to secure a bag."

"Then once we get back to the Mil later tonight, let's hit up the club so I can drop a bag on Nina," Phat grinned. "And Sonny Boy can meet us there, so me and him can handle our business. That way I'll be able to take care of two things at the same damn time."

"I'm with that," Ace agreed.

Subsequent to Phat dealing with his plug, he and Ace n'em decided to grab a bite to eat before heading back to their hometown. They pulled up to a popular spot, Harold's, located on the south side of town in Englewood, well-known for its fried chicken., This particular chicken joint is a hotspot favored by Chicagoans. Troy parked the BMW curbside in front of the restaurant. The group noticed there were numerous patrons, niggas and bitches alike, running in and out of the place. And the fact that the city was known for its homicides heightened their senses.

"Troy, you stay in the whip, and keep the engine runnin'. We'll be in and out," Phat made clear as he put the FN 5.6 on his waist.

"A'ight. Just grab me a chicken sammich," Troy requested. He had twin .9 Glocks with thirty-shot clips in lap.

"I'ma stay back with Troy and secure the whip," Nice piped in. His hand rested on the choppa in his lap.

"Cool," Phat concurred, especially since there were kilos in the truck that he had just copped from his plug. He looked over to Ace. "Let's be on point out here. These Chiraq niggas lookin' real hungry."

Ace pocketed his .45 Glock fixed with a thirty-two-shot clip and a converter switch, then quipped, "I'm hungry too, so let's go and grab somethin' to eat real quick."

Once they stepped out of the whip, Ace and Phat made their way inside of Harold's. While awaiting to place their orders, Ace peeped a few mu'fuckas gawking at Phat's chain and watch, both bust-down with diamonds. After placing their orders and receiving the food to go, Ace and Phat headed out of the chicken joint.

As the two approached the whip, suddenly a dread-head nigga that was posted outside started to advance on them with a Tec-9 in hand. Once Ace peeped Dread-Head, he turned and upped his .45, in a motion almost too fast to follow, then the two matched guns.

Boc! Boc! Boc! Boc! Boc! Boc!

Prraat! Prraat!

The two simultaneously shot at one another, Ace's Glock shot rapidly like a mini choppa and struck Dread-Head five times in the chest, causing Dread-Head's shots to miss wildly and strike the hood of the BMW. Ace left Dread-Head stretched out on the sidewalk, bleeding profusely and choking to death on his own blood.

Phat hurried into the backseat of the BMW and Ace followed suit. Before they could even shut the door, Troy skirted away from the curb with Nice watching the rearview mirror for any tails. Needing to get the hell out of town, they were fleeing back to Milwaukee on Highway I-94.

**

Seated near that main stage in the strip club, Ace n'em watched a bad-ass redbone bitch execute pole tricks. As planned, once they got back to the Mil later that night, they hit up the club, mainly to see Savvy and Nina. And Sonny Boy was present also, he met them there, after Phat had called him to come through. Ace had offered Chedda to show up, but Chedda declined and advised Ace he best not get too close to Phat. While they were at the club, the group popped bottles and gave strippers money showers.

"Listen, Ace," Phat began, "that was all love what you did back in the Chi. Nigga almost caught my ass slippin'."

Ace put the bottle of Ace of Spade up to his lips, then replied, "Only did what I was paid to do. That's all." He wanted it to be known that what he had done wasn't out of love. "So, don't mention it."

"Fa sho." Phat could read that Ace was guarded. Seething, he thought, *fuck is this nigga problem?*

46

"So, what's the deal with the work?" Sonny Boy piped in, speaking to Phat. He took a puff from the blunt of cookie weed.

"I'll make sure you leave here with it. You just make sure I get paid," Phat told him.

"No problem."

"Now, let's get lit." Phat noticed Nina, then he tried waving her over with a stack of hundreds. She held up her index finger for him to wait. Instead, he went chasing after her.

Ace shook his head at how Phat was sweating a bitch that clearly didn't want his fat-ass. Looking around the club, he didn't see the pimp nigga, Toucan present, but some of his hoes were working. Ace wondered how Toucan was able to pimp on so many bad bitches. While he sat there taking in the scene, Savvy came and sat in his lap. She grabbed the bottle from him, turned it up to her lips.

"You coming home with me tonight, Zaddy?" Sav asked, seductively.

"Yeah. Now go and make us some money," Ace told her. He smacked her ass as she strutted away.

Once a thick-ass white bitch announced by the DJ as Bunny, took to the main stage, she started putting on a terrific show to Mulatto's tune "On God." Her hair was red and cut low with designs, she was covered in tatts, and she only wore red lace lingerie and stilettos. Sonny grabbed his money-gun, approached the stage then triggered crisp bills into the air that rained down all over Bunny. She got on all fours and popped her pussy, then other ballers began showering her with cash.

She's the type of bitch we'll need in our club, Ace mused. He'd keep Bunny in mind.

Meanwhile, a nigga named Blue, followed by his right-hand man, Forty, who were both dripped in ice on their necks and wrists, entered the strip club looking to enjoy themselves. But that thought abruptly came to an end when Forty pointed out Sonny Boy, who was making it rain. The two approached Sonny Boy. Ace noticed how Sonny and Blue mean-mugged each other once their eyes met. He didn't know who the fuck the nigga was, but Ace could sense tension in the air. He was patient but ready to brawl.

"Sonny Boy, I wasn't expectin' to bump into you here. Guess you got money to blow, now that your pockets are fat," Blue sniped.

"Never count a nigga pockets thinkin' you deserve it," Sonny Boy remarked as Ace stood by his side.

"Whatever. Listen, word in the hood is you got a problem with how I'm servin' my work."

"Naw, my problem is with you servin' your work to my clientele. Blue, you know you're gettin' in the way of my paper, and I ain't gon' warn your ass again to find your own fuckin' clients to serve."

"Nigga, all you gotta do is cash me out and I'll fall back," Blue bargained.

"You don't got shit else comin' from me. Already gave your ass back double that light shit you had left me with," Sonny retorted.

"Think just 'cause you got a lil cheese now, you don't need me? You wouldn't even have shit if it wasn't 'cause of me leavin' your ass with my fuckin' stash!"

"I ain't never need shit from you, nigga. So, miss me with that!"

Blue stepped into Sonny's personal space. "Blood or not, you can get some smoke too," he warned, pointing a finger in Sonny's face.

Sonny Boy pushed Blue's hand away and stated, "Don't fuck around and get yourself hurt, bro."

"Say no more, nigga." Blue turned and headed out of the club with Forty in tow.

While watching the niggas walk away, Ace suggested, "We can go and dump them niggas down, right now."

"Naw, homeboy. I'ma take care of the shit some other way," Sonny Boy told him as Blue and Forty exited.

"Who the fuck is dude n'em anyway?" Ace sipped at his bottle of Ace of Spade as he and Sonny Boy took their seats.

"Blue is my half-brotha, same dad. And ever since Blue got outta fed prison, me and him haven't been seein' eye-to-eye, due to problems over money. 'Cause when he went to do a two-year bid in the feds, he had left me with twenty-five G's and nine ounces of coke. Then once Blue returned home, I showed his ass love by givin' him fifty G's and a half-brick of crack as compensation.

"But Blue feels like he's entitled to half of my stash, since I ran it up, usin' the paper and work he had left me. And once I denied bro, then the nigga started to feel some type of way towards me. So, him and his goofy-ass homeboy Forty, the nigga that was just with him, has been tryin' to swipe all of my clientele and fuck up my money," Sonny expounded.

"Listen, my dude, you gotta set an example, or them niggas just gon' keep tryin' you. And it seems to me like if you don't cash out your bro, then he ain't finna fall back," Ace laid out. He passed the bottle to Sonny.

Taking a gulp of the champagne, Sonny needed a drink right about now. "That shit dead, I ain't cashin' out Blue," he stated. Sonny had deadly motives.

Phat returned to the table after chasing down Nina. "Everything a'ight?"

"Yeah, it ain't shit," Sonny Boy told him. "Now, let's get back to gettin' lit."

Martell "Troublesome" Bolden

Chapter 6

The Audi yielded in the middle of the street with Chedda behind the wheel and a stick in his lap. He was stopping to scoop up Ace. It was close to noon, and they had to go and make a serve. Chedda texted Ace that he was outside, a moment later Ace emerged from his side-bitch crib then made his way towards the whip. Once Ace stepped into the passenger seat, Chedda dipped off down the street, playing YFN Lucci's tune, "Big Ole."

"What's to it, my boy?" Chedda greeted and passed his boy the Sprite soda bottle mixed with lean.

"You tell me." Ace took a sip of the dirty Sprite.

"Gotta go and dump this brick real quick."

"Who you finna serve that brick to?"

"Rex. About to meet up with him at Wendy's."

"I'ont know why you be servin' dawg, 'cause he seems suspect."

"Been servin' him for a minute, and shit been all good," Chedda said as he yielded at a stoplight on National Street. "Speakin' of servin' someone, heard you put on Kiki. Whassup with that?"

"Lil sis had hollered at me about it, and I can see she got it in her to run it up harder than most niggas. She already got my lil bro's money-phone, so she won't have a problem with gettin' off the work," Ace responded. He sipped the lean once more, then passed it back to his boy.

Chedda took a gulp of the purple syrup. "I just don't want shit to happen to her, 'cause we both know how savage this game is."

"I feel you, my nigga. Especially after what happened with Neesha, I still haven't gotten over that shit. Yeah, Kiki may be pretty but she's a savage. Gee groomed her ass the right way."

"A'ight. Just watch after lil sis."

"Fa sho," Ace assured him. He changed the subject. "Nigga, why the fuck your ass didn't pull up to the club last night? That bitch was lit!"

"I was too busy makin' serves, while you was out gettin' lit and shit with that weak-ass nigga, Phat. Plus, you know I'ont fuck with dawg fat-ass like that. And you need to be careful fuckin' with him," Chedda replied, indifferently.

"Yeah, I know. Had to fuck around and drop a nigga in Chiraq yesterday 'cause of him."

"Straight up?"

"Straight up. And his two so-called shooters were there but didn't do shit. Both of them niggas some hoes. Only reason I even hit the club with Phat n'em last night is 'cause my nigga Sonny Boy was there too. But we gon' start servin' bro weight so he don't have to deal with Phat again."

"Say no more," Chedda said. The light flipped green, and he pulled off with traffic, driving real smooth with the pie in the car in order to avoid twelve. "Speakin' of clubs, the lawyer finalized the paperwork for us to go ahead and open our own shit."

"That's whassup!" Ace exclaimed, rubbing his palms together.

In between Ace making serves and making cutthroat moves, he had invested in the strip club venture with Chedda. By now Chedda had found a nice spot located in the inner city that would be best for them to open the club, he was in charge of handling all of the legal work in order to make their business legitimate, so he was consistently in talks with a lawyer on their behalf. And Ace was in charge of seeing to it that the club be employed by some of the baddest bitches, so he was in cahoots with Savvy on that task.

"We need ten more G's apiece to pay off legal fees," Chedda let him know. He passed the half bottle of dirty Sprite to his right.

"No problem. That shit light," Ace replied. He imbibed some of the thick drink.

"Have you found any bad bitches to work for us yet?"

"Still workin' on it. But I got an idea of how to find some, if the plan with Savvy don't work for us."

"A'ight. We'll be holdin' auditions for the girls soon. And the spot I picked out is gonna be good for business. It's located on 35th and Hampton Street."

"Now that we have all of that shit in order, what're we gon' name the club?" Ace inquired. "I was thinkin' about Baddies." He sipped the wock then handed the bottle to Chedda.

"Baddies." Chedda let the name roll over in his head as he drank some lean.

"Yeah, I like it. Next, we gotta start fixin' up the place. Then in a few months we'll be open for business, and we won't have to worry much about catchin' a drug case," he said as he swirled the mixture around in the soda bottle.

"Good. 'Cause bad enough we gotta worry about catchin' a body. That's why we have to smoke the bitch-ass nigga, Stone," Ace added. Since Gee's murder, Ace was beefin' heavily with Stone, over the past few months several bodies had been dropping on either side.

"I feel you, my boy. Stone's the main reason why we have so much beef right now," Chedda agreed. "But we haven't been able to catch the nigga Stone lately, 'cause his bitch ass don't be in the hood as much. At least now we got the hood on lock."

"Yeah, our niggas got plenty of straps and is flooded with work. Even still, I ain't gon' let Stone ass get away with killin' Gee. I'ma be sure to keep lil bro name alive in these streets." It was hard on Ace to have lost Gee, especially being that Ace felt it was his own fuckin' fault.

"I'm with you on that, fa sho. But even while we're in beef, there's still money to be made. Only problem is gettin' money and beefin' don't mix well." Chedda returned the soda bottle to Ace.

"And as long as the bodies keeps droppin', then twelve gon' keep sweatin' the hood, makin' it a problem for us to move yae. So, we need to whack Stone ASAP in order to stop so much of the beef and prevent twelve from slowin' up our paper."

"The beef has been so real, the crooked-ass cop Lucas is snatchin' up plenty of mu'fuckas, even if he have to plant drugs and guns on 'em. But more than anyone, Lucas wants you, Ace."

"Yeah, I know. Heard that mu'fucka been pressin' people from around the hood to snitch on me about some homies and shit. But no one will cooperate. Ever since that night I had busted at him, Lucas is determined to put my ass under prison. But I ain't goin' back to prison no matter what." Ace took a gulp of the purple syrup.

"And I'ont wanna have to send your ass any more cash for canteen and shit," Chedda half-joked, and the two busted out laughing. "But on some real nigga shit, once we get rich the legit way, then we won't have to worry about twelve. Especially the feds."

"At least we'll be flexin' hard as hell if the feds watchin'!" Ace smirked.

"Big facts. Which is why as soon as I dump off this brick, we gon' hit up the jeweler. And in a couple days we can take a trip to Texas and have Johnny Dang flood our mouths with permanent gold teeth and diamonds."

"A'ight. I'll drop a bag on some jewels. Plus, I just copped a foreign whip I been waitin' to pull out." Since Ace had run it up over time, he wanted to show niggas how to get their glaze on.

"Nigga, watch what fat whip I pull out when the summertime hit!"

Ace sipped the dirty Sprite one last time before passing what was left in the soda bottle to his boy. "Let's just remember all of the paper, jewelry, and whips don't make niggas real."

"That's real nigga shit." Chedda downed the rest of the lean.

Arriving at Wendy's, Chedda pulled his Audi into the parking lot of the restaurant and parked beside the light gray Range Rover. The nigga Rex stepped out the Range looked around perpetually, then entered the backseat of the Audi. This was only the second time Ace had the chance to be around Rex, and like the first time, he thought the nigga seemed to be acting 'noid and shit. Ace gripped the switch in his lap, just in case. After Chedda made the drug transaction with Rex the two dapped, then Rex exited the car and entered his truck, going on his way.

"I'm tellin' you, fam', buddy suspect. Nigga barely talked to you, let alone made any eye contact," Ace pointed out.

Chedda thumbed through the bands he'd just accumulated from the serve, and told him, "My nigga, I only need to hear the money talk." He stuffed the bundle of cash in the pocket of his Off-White jeans. "Now stop trippin' and let's go grab somethin' to eat real quick. That drank got a nigga with the munchies like a mu'fucka."

Before stepping out of the Audi, Ace stuffed his Glock on his waist and Chedda did the same. Inside the fast-food joint, the two waited to place their orders to go. While awaiting their food orders to be fulfilled, Dre and one of his niggas entered the restaurant. As soon as Ace saw Dre, he immediately recognized him as being Savvy's lil brotha. Keepin' it a hunnit, Ace didn't really like the nigga, but on the strength of Savvy, he let Dre slide before. But he wouldn't let his ass slide twice.

Ace offered Dre a head nod, but Dre held a mean-mug. He peeped how Dre leaned towards the tall, skinny, light-skinned nigga that accompanied him and whispered something to him. He couldn't help but notice Dre and his boy muggin' him, and for their observation, Ace readjusted the switch on his waist as a forewarning that tryin' him would get a nigga popped quick. Whole time, Chedda peeped what was taking place, but he played shit cool. When Chedda collected their bag of fast food, Ace followed his boy out the restaurant.

As they approached the Audi, Chedda asked, "Who the fuck was them niggas?"

"Man, one of them bum-ass niggas is just Savvy's lil brotha. And lil dawg ain't on shit," Ace told him as they entered the car.

"Well, his ass was actin' like he on that."

Ace scoffed. "Dawg just salty I'm fuckin' his sis, that's all."

"You really fuck with Savvy, huh?" Chedda raised a brow at him. He push-started the whip, then pulled out of the lot into traffic.

"I like that shorty accepts bein' my side-bitch, even knowin' Paris is not only my main bitch, but also my BM. Although I can tell at times she wants more with me, even still she respects what I have with Paris. And Sav just plays her role the way a nigga need her to, 'cause she understands my ambition to run it up in the streets," Ace expounded.

"That's whassup. But what about Paris?" Chedda played devil's advocate.

"Even though I'm vibin' with Savvy as much as I am, me and Paris is in a good place. I like spendin' time with her and Adonis. However, she wants more of my time, 'cause she feels like I've been spendin' most of it chasin' a bag. But I need her ass to understand I'm out here in the streets runnin' up some commas to take care of home."

"Listen, my nigga. Even though I be fuckin' off on Antoinette, I make sure she knows she's wifey. Sometimes we gotta do shit to show our main bitch she's worthy," Chedda jeweled him. "Feel me?"

"Yeah, I feel you, my nigga." Ace felt where his niggas was coming from and would be sure to take heed. Because even though he fucked with Savvy the long way, it was Paris he wanted to be with for the long haul. He added, "I see you, droppin' jewels and shit."

Chedda glanced over at him with a smirk. "Just like I'm finna drop some jewels around my neck."

While heading to their next destination, they grubbed on their Wendy's meals. And they rapped about how the game was so fucked up nowadays, due to niggas snitchin' and backdoorin', and bitches schemin' and sack-chasin'. They came to the conclusion that the rules of the game don't change, just the players do. And Ace and Chedda were playing for keeps.

Arriving at Pak's jewelry shop, Chedda veered his Audi to the curb and parked in front of the establishment. He and Ace hopped out of the whip, then approached the locked entrance door and had to be buzzed in. Inside, while Ace and Chedda checked out the collection of jewelry displayed in the glass showcases, there were some ballin'-ass niggas and bitches also shopping around. Soon thereafter, Ace and Chedda were approached by Geno, the jeweler.

"Need some help with anything?" Geno offered, with his foreign accent noticeable.

"Yeah. Lemme get these boogers and that bitch right there," Chedda requested, pointing out some diamond earrings and a gold choke-chain with a huge cross pendant that was flooded with diamonds. "What that shit gon' run me?"

"Excellent choices. For the earrings, nine hundred fifty. And twenty-four thousand for the chain here."

"Bet. Run it."

The jeweler sat the items aside and then turned to Ace. "See anything you like?"

"Just that mu'fucka right there." Ace pointed out a gold Rolex timepiece with diamonds circling its face. "Nice. It'll cost you twenty-two grand."

"Say no more." Ace had thirty racks in his pocket.

"Anything else I can help you two fellas with?" Geno wanted to know.

Chedda upped his bankroll and replied, "We only got cash. So, is it cool if we cash you out without callin' attention to ourselves by the feds and shit?"

"Sure, no problem. However, I'll have to tax you extra for the inconvenience. Let's say, a grand each."

"We got you," Ace piped in and agreed.

"You heard my nigga. Now bag that shit up," Chedda added.

Geno, the jeweler, was known for dealing with mainly trap gods, like Ace and Chedda. So, for a fee, he often pulled strings for his clients in order to cover up their ill-gained riches and deceive the alphabet boys.

Collectively, they cashed out about fifty G's on their jewelry. All of Ace's life, he had hustled just to get the moola, now he had stacked up his change, and was able to go see the jeweler. But no amount of money or diamonds would change him.

Martell "Troublesome" Bolden

Chapter 7

Catchin' plays off his money-phone, Ace pushed the Acura through the evening traffic, after servin' yet another buyer. Thus far today, he had run up close to ten racks. When his iPhone rang, he looked down at it in the cupholder and saw the call was from Sonny Boy. He grabbed up the phone and answered.

"What it do, fool?"

"Shit. Out here chasin' a bag," Sonny Boy replied.

"You and me both," Ace said.

"No doubt. You got some more of that loud on deck?"

"Always."

"I'ma pull up on you then. Wanna holla at you 'bout some shit anyway," Sonny Boy mentioned.

"I'm in traffic right now," Ace told him as he dipped around a minivan. "My nigga, just meet me at the L-store in my hood in like twenty mins." He wrapped up the call.

While Ace pushed the Acura, he rapped along to Peezy's tune "Exhausted." Going eastbound on Center Street, he was headed to meet up with Sonny Boy in the hood. Sonny Boy usually hit him up for some loud, but this time around Ace could tell something was up by the tone of his voice. As Ace shifted through traffic, he contemplated, *I'm sure whatever my nigga wanna holla at me about is a money move.*

Once Ace made it to the hood, he stopped at the liquor store. He didn't see Sonny Boy's whip there yet. Before stepping out the car, Ace stuffed the Glock in the front pocket of his Gucci skinny jeans. Inside the L-store, Ace went to the front counter, where Abdul stood behind the cash register dealing with patrons and Ace awaited them paying for their items.

"Abdul, my guy, whassup?" Ace greeted as he stepped up to make his purchase when it was his turn.

"I'm alright. How you?" Abdul said.

"I'm good. Lemme get a fifth of Hennessy." He lay a twenty on the counter for the bottle of liquor.

Abdul grabbed the dub and placed it in the register, then handed over the bottle to him. "Your sister was actually in here a moment ago with her little boy. I caught him trying to steal some candy, and I told him all he has to do is ask me for anything. Mika wanted to whoop his ass, but I told her it wasn't necessary."

"Good lookin' for takin' it easy on my nephew. But you shoulda kicked his lil ass," Ace half-joked.

"He reminds me of your little brother, Gee, when he was that age. Gee used to come in here and steal snacks all the time and didn't think I knew, but I just would look the other way." Abdul chuckled. "That little brother of yours turned out to be a good dude. It's fucked up what happened to him," he said sympathetically.

"Yeah, lil bro was one-hunnit. On his grave, I'ma slide on Stone for that shit," Ace vowed. "But that pussy-ass nigga ain't been in the hood much since the shit happened. Listen, if that pussy nigga have the heart to bring his ass in here, hit me up and let me know ASAP."

"Certainly. And if you need any firearms, I can get you some big shit. Check this one out." Abdul came up from under the counter with a MK-18 assault-rifle.

"On Gee, that bitch fat!" Ace admired the weapon. "A'ight, I'ma cop some shit from you."

"Just come back when you need some, and we'll talk then," Abdul told him as he put the gun away.

"Fa sho."

A patron entered the liquor store, it was Sonny Boy. He approached Ace, and said, "My bad for runnin' late, but I had to make a couple serves. You know how that shit goes."

"It's all good, boss. I just pulled up here not too long myself," Ace replied.

"Look, lemme cop myself a box of blunts real quick and I'ma holla at you outside."

"A'ight."

As Ace headed outside with the bottle of Henny in hand he overheard Sonny Boy ask Abdul for a box of Backwoods blunts. While standing in front of the L-store, Ace's iPhone chimed a text message. He pulled out the phone and read the text from Sly, which was for Ace to stop by the trap house to pick up some money. Ace was finna send a text in reply but yielded when Sonny Boy stepped out of the store.

"Let's jump in my whip and rap," Sonny Boy suggested. He stepped into his Audi SUV, then Ace followed and entered the passenger seat. "Lemme get a zip of that smoke."

"Just gimme a hundred and fifty bucks." Ace pulled out the Ziploc from the pocket of his hoodie and handed over an ounce. Sonny Boy held the weed to his nostrils and smelled its strong aroma. "This shit smells loud!"

"All I move is that loud pack."

"Fa sho." Sonny Boy grabbed a bankroll that was in his cup holder and counted out the cash, then paid Ace. He then began splitting the seams of a blunt to roll up and said, "Listen, the shit I wanna holla you about has to do with Blue and his nigga, Forty. They been fuckin' with my paper by servin' some of my clientele weight for dirt cheap. I want you to make an example outta Forty, lay down that nigga and make sure he stay down. Feel me?"

"Yeah, I feel you. But what's in it for me?" Ace inquired.

"Heard the nigga's up like three birds and at least a hunnit bands. You can keep all of that shit for yourself." Sonny Boy dashed down the window some then dumped the tobacco from within the blunt outside onto the ground. "So, you down?"

"Yeah, I'm down. Tell me what you know about this nigga."

"The nigga be on 36th and Fairmont Street in the only blue house on the block, and he push a purple Chevy Camaro on rims. That's all I know right now." After filling the blunt with buds of weed, Sonny Boy began rolling it up.

"A'ight. Just leave the nigga to me, and I'ma lay his ass down," Ace assured. "What about Blue?"

"Leave his ass alone for now. I'll deal with him."

"You got that."

They shook up before Ace stepped out of the whip, and Sonny Boy lit his blunt before he dispelled down the street. Ace entered the Acura and then drove around the corner to the trap spot. He parked and remained sitting inside the whip. He texted Sly that he was outside and a moment later, Sly emerged from the trap and then made his way into the passenger seat.

"Damn, you pulled up quick," Sly noted as he handed over a bundle of flip money. "That's eight G's."

Ace placed the bundle in the cupholder and said, "I was only around the corner at the L-store for a minute." He blessed his bottle of liquor before opening it and taking a swig.

"What were you doin' there?"

"Besides coppin' a bottle of Henny, I was hollerin' at one of my niggas 'bout some shit. Matter fact, you strapped?"

"Glizzy with a stick." Sly took his Glock .26 fitted with an extended clip off his waist and sat it on his lap. "Why, whaddup?"

Ace started the car. "We finna go on this move real quick," he told him as they dispelled away from the curb.

Sitting in the Acura while strapped up, Ace and Sly staked out the only blue house located on 36th and Fairmount Street from down the block. They were waiting on Forty. After Sonny Boy had put Ace on Forty, Ace set out to find out where he lay his head and lay Forty down tonight. An half hour had passed before Ace peeped Forty's purple Chevrolet Camaro turn onto the block. He looked on as the Camaro parked in front of a blue duplex home, then a short, stocky, dark skinned nigga with braids stepped out, who was Forty. Ace noticed his neck was bust-down with diamonds, and he peeped the nigga adjust a pipe on his waist. From observation he noticed that there was no one else inside of the house, or there was no one riding with Forty.

"There the nigga is right there," Ace pointed out. He gripped firmly on the .45 Glock fitted with a thirty-two-shot stick and a converter switch. "Since he's by himself, I got his ass. Just sit in the whip and be ready to bounce." After tossing his hoodie up over his head, Ace slipped out of the car with gun in hand, then he crept down the block that was dimly lit by the only few working streetlights.

As Forty headed towards the front door of the house he was oblivious to the imminent threat advancing on him from behind. He climbed the porch steps and once he slid his key into the door lock, he felt a barrel pressed to the nape of his neck. Forty was tempted to make a move for his own gun.

"Listen here, nigga, if you move I'ma shoot your mu'fuckin' head off," Ace forewarned, menacingly. He frisked Forty and took a .40 caliber off his waist, then stuck it in his own pocket. "Now, slowly unlock the door and take me to the stash."

"I know Sonny Boy sent you, and—"

Whack!

Ace slapped Forty upside his head with the Glock, cutting his words short. "Bitch, shut the fuck up and do what I told your ass!"

With no further words, Forty did what he was told. Once the door was unlocked, Ace walked him inside while holding the back of Forty's shirt collar, with the barrel pressed to the back of his skull. Suddenly, Forty managed to break away from Ace's hold and ran for the back door. Ace chased him down while bustin'.

Boc! Boc! Boc! Boc! Boc!

Two slugs hit Forty in his back—one of them punctured a lung. He staggered then collapsed, feeling like his insides was on fire. "A'ight, a'ight! That sh-shit in the b-bedroom."

"C'mon, stupid-ass nigga." Ace grabbed Forty's shirt and practically dragged him to the bedroom. "Where the fuck it's at?"

"It's in... th-the... lower dr-dresser," Forty managed to get out in between ragged breaths. It hurt for him to breathe.

"Open it up and lemme see." Ace stood back, holding Forty at gunpoint while he pulled open the dresser, inside there was some packaged cocaine and plenty stacks of cash wrapped with rubber bands. "A'ight. Now lay the fuck down, and don't move," Ace demanded.

Once Forty was lying face-down on the floor, Ace grabbed a pillowcase and began tossing the coke and money inside of it. After ransacking the rest of the room, he only found an AR-15 beneath the mattress and placed the weapon inside of the pillowcase. When Ace looked over at Forty, he then realized the nigga was no longer breathing. Forty had succumbed to the slugs he had taken. Ace stripped the bust-down Cuban link chain from the neck of a dead Forty, also tossing it into the pillowcase. Getting what he had come for, Ace hurried out the front door.

Ace emerged from the duplex home with his switch in one hand and the pillowcase containing the merch in his other. There was now a small crowd of people formed on the block, wanting to witness what the hell was going on after hearing the gunfire. Once Sly saw Ace, then he pulled up. As Ace hurried towards the car, he aimed the Glock at the crowd of onlookers and caused them to immediately disburse. Once Ace jumped into the passenger seat, he tossed the pillowcase into the backseat then sat both of the handguns on his lap as Sly skirted off.

During the ride back to the hood, Ace gave Sly a play-by-play of what happened, and they joked and laughed about the shit while sharing the bottle of liquor. As Sly pushed the whip, Ace pulled out his phone to send a text.

ACE:

That shit done.

A second later, Ace received a text from Sonny Boy. He read it.

SONNY:

Enough said.

Now Ace and Sonny Boy's business was squared away.

Once Sly pulled up on the block, he parked in front of the trap house. "You need me for anything else?"

"Naw. Here, take this for ridin' with me." Ace grabbed the bundle of cash from the cup holder then returned it to Sly, along with the .40 caliber he had confiscated from a now-dead Forty.

"Good lookin', homeboy."

After they shook up, Sly stepped out of the car and Ace jumped over the middle console into the driver's seat. Ace drove away as Sly made his way into the trap.

Ace drove to Savvy's crib. He turned into the alley and parked behind the house. Before stepping out of the car, he pocketed his pole then reached into the backseat and grabbed the pillowcase. He approached the back door and entered the house then locked the door behind himself. Since Savvy was out working at the club tonight, he was there alone. Ace went into the front room, where he placed his two iPhones, keys, and gun on the end table. Noticing a half-smoked blunt in the ashtray, he grabbed the blunt then flamed it up, and took a seat on the couch.

Ace dumped the contents out of the pillowcase atop the coffee table. He put the diamond chain on the end table also. After separating the money and drugs into two piles, Ace began to count it all up. By hand, he counted a hundred-thirty-three G's and weighed up over two keys altogether. He then put it all away inside the hidden compartment with the rest of his stash. Ace continued his ambition to get rich the savage way.

Chapter 8

While at home, Ace was chillin' with Adonis, since Paris was out and about running errands. Ace always enjoyed spending time with his son, whenever he wasn't out in the streets trappin'. He knew Paris preferred him to be home more with her and Adonis, even though Ace was taking care of home. And without a doubt Ace loved his BM, he just couldn't seem to give her the life she wanted with him, due to his living the street life. Although he was there for them and wanted to show Paris what she and his son meant to him.

Ace and Adonis were in the front room seated on the couch. Both of them were wearing only tank-tops and basketball shorts, while eating junk-food and watching *The Black Panther*. After finishing their ice cream, Ace took the bowls into the kitchen and placed them inside the dishwasher. While he looked inside of the fridge, Adonis followed his dad into the kitchen.

"Daddy, me gotta pee-pee," Adonis said in his broken English, holding his crotch.

"C'mon." Ace led his son to the bathroom for some potty training. He pulled down Adonis's basketball shorts and Pull-Ups, then taught him to stand in front of his potty and said, "Now go ahead and pee, like a big boy."

"Me a big boy now, Daddy!" Adonis peed into the potty for the most part, some of his pee splashed the floor.

"Yeah, you a big boy. So, anytime you gotta pee, then do it just like I taught you." Ace was proud to be teaching his son things a pops should. Things that unfortunately, his own pops wasn't available to teach him while growing up. Because Ace loss his pops to the street life, at such a young age, and he didn't want Adonis to lose him the same. But the reality is he lived the street nigga lifestyle, so it wasn't a guarantee he would make it home to his son. One thing for sure, Ace wasn't a deadbeat dad.

Ace had Adonis wash his toddler hands, while Ace cleaned up the pee on the floor. Hearing his iPhone ring, Ace made his way into the front room with Adonis on his heels. He sat his son on the couch, then took a seat himself. Grabbing his phone off the end table, Ace saw on the display it was a collect call from his mom, Gale. After losing Glen, Ace and Gale seemed to grow closer than ever before. Lately, he had been talking with her via phone. Also, he consistently gave Mika pictures and money to send their mom, because he knew how it was to be on lockdown. But Ace knew his mama was strong.

"How you, Ma?" Ace said once the collect call connected after he'd accepted it.

"I'm fine, son," Gale replied cheerfully. "And you?"

"I'm good. Just chillin' with Adonis while Paris is gone."

"Lemme talk to my grandbaby, with his cute self."

"Don't let that cute shit fool you, 'cause lil dude bad." Ace handed the phone to his son, and told him, "Your granny wanna talk to you."

"Hi, Gwanny!" Adonis was always excited to talk with Gale whenever he got a chance to.

"Hey, little man. I can't wait to hug and kiss you!"

"Me too. You gon' buy me some toys?"

"Only if you being a good boy."

"Okay. Daddy said he gon' whoop me ass if me be bad," Adonis said, parroting what Ace had warned him before.

"Boy, I'ma be the one to whoop your butt if you cuss again," Gale responded. "Granny love you so much. Now lemme talk to your daddy."

Ace grabbed the phone back. "Lil homie somethin' else," he told his mom, chuckling.

"His ass reminds me so much of you. And from the pictures Mika sent me, he favors you and your brother a lot. Ace, I'm so proud of you for being there for your son. Every little boy needs a dad in their life, so you don't want to end up like yours did."

"You right. 'Cause knowin' a nigga smoked my pops, that shit made me upset. I was five years old then, but it made me man up. Ma, I was the man of the house and had to figure shit out the times you went to the feds. So, without you and my pops, the streets raised me," he expressed.

Gale exhaled deeply. "It's fucked up you, your sister and brother, had to go through that. But real men stand tall, they don't never fall. Now do what you have to in order to hold your sister down and feed your family."

"I hear you. And when you come home, I'ma make sure you don't need for shit. Real talk, I'm out here doin' my all to get rich in these streets."

"Just make sure you don't end up in the feds like me, or in an early grave like your dad."

"One thing's fa sho, I'll take my loss either way without snitchin' or foldin'. Guess I got your hustle, and I got my pops' heart."

"Yeah, you do. However, do it better than me and him. Watch the niggas you deal with and don't trust many bitches. 'Cause it ain't what you do, it's how you do it." She shared some game with him.

"That's real, Ma."

"You may be a savage in them streets, but to me, you're still my son."

The automated voice intervened and warned them there was one minute remaining on the collect call. Ace and Gale said their goodbyes before hanging up. Though his mama hadn't been there for him and his siblings much at all, Ace did want her to at least have a chance to be in her grandkids' lives. Admittedly, he felt a need to forgive her and mend their bond.

While Adonis had fallen asleep watching the movie, Ace scrolled down his news feed on *Facebook* to see what was going on. He saw Poppa and Bookie had posted some flexed-up pictures, he thought, *lil bro n'em stay flexin' hard*. And there was a video of Savvy twerkin' her ass in the camera. He introspectively said, *she definitely knows how to throw that ass*. Then, he couldn't help but notice the video of an unarmed Black man being shot to death by a cop, he contemplated, *damn, Black people can't even breathe around cops without bein' killed*. But what caught his eye was Duke and some of Stone's niggas', posts about how they were gonna smoke Ace. He scoffed, and mused, *those niggas ain't on shit*.

It was a quarter to nine pm when Paris came into the crib. She kicked off her Air Force Ones at the door while carrying a bag of groceries. Adonis remained asleep on the couch as Ace went to assist her with the grocery bag. She asked him to go and get the other bags out of the car, and he did so. Ace sat three more bags on the island in the kitchen and began helping Paris put the groceries away.

"How was he while I was out?" Paris inquired about their son while placing a carton of eggs in the fridge.

"He's always good whenever he's with me," Ace told her.

"Maybe he needs you more. And so do I."

"Listen, Paris. I may be in the streets a lot but at least I take care of home." He handed Paris a box of Froot Loops and she put it away in the cabinet.

"True. Even still, it's one thing to take care of home and it's another to bring your ass home every night, Ace." She eyed him through slits.

"I know some nights I'ont come to the crib, but that's 'cause I'm out chasin' a bag with no sleep."

"Well, lemme find out it's because you're really sleeping in another bitch bed," Paris forewarned.

Though Ace's relationship with Savvy had grown close, he and Paris were in a good place. He liked spending time with Paris and his son. However, she wanted more of his time because she felt as though Ace had been spending most of it doing who knows what. But he needed her to understand he was out on the grind, doing whatever he needed to do in order to make sure they were good. Like Savvy, Ace really needed Paris to understand his ambition to get rich or die tryin'.

Ace pulled Paris into his chest. "Only bitch that matters is you." He kissed her lips and palmed her ass.

"Ace, would you please stop, before you start something you can't finish." Her pussy was moist.

"Adonis is in there sleep, so I can finish whatever I start."

Paris didn't try to stop Ace once he grabbed her hand and led her towards their bedroom. They were careful not to awake Adonis on their way through the front room. Once inside their bedroom, Ace undid her skinny jeans and helped her out of them, along with the panty-thong she wore beneath. He stepped out of his shorts, freeing his hard dick.

Dropping onto her knees, Paris sucked and licked on the tip of his hardness. She worked her soft lips and warm mouth back and forth on him, while Ace watched her do her thang!

"Damn, girl. Some head like this gon' get your ass whatever you want. This shit got a nigga ready to bust a nut," Ace grunted. Not wanting to nut just yet, he pulled Paris onto her feet, then he sat back on the edge of the bed. "Climb on me."

Paris climbed on his lap as instructed, then Ace guided his long, hard pipe inside her tight, wet slit. She bounced up and down on the dick while he grasped her ass in both hands.

Her pussy was so wet it made fart sounds as she rode his joint. The feeling of Ace's dick deep in her guts drove her wild!

"Yaaas, Ace. Baby...this dick is so damn big!" Paris moaned loudly.

"Shhh, before you wake up Adonis," Ace warned in a lowered voice.

"I'm...I'm cummin," she whispered as her pussy exploded! Ace stood up from the bed while holding Paris, then lay her back on the edge of the bed. While standing, he pushed her knees back to her chest and drilled his piece back and forth inside her slit. Ace was balls deep in the pussy when he felt himself finna bust a nut. Her pussy felt so damn tight and good, he didn't pull his dick out as he reached climax. Being weak in the knees, Ace lay in bed beside Paris, both worn out from their quickie.

"Told your ass I can finish what I start," Ace commented.

"Boy, shut up," Paris giggled. "Speaking of, I gotta finish putting away groceries." She put on some sweatpants then left the room.

While Ace lay back in bed, he thought about what he and Chedda had talked about a few days back. And he had to admit his boy was right, he needed to make sure Paris knew she was the most important girl to him. So, he had a way of proving to her how much he loved and trusted her. She was there for him when he had gotten popped up, when he was in prison, and when he was flat broke. Shit, she deserved for him to do good by her, after all of the shit Paris had been through with his ass. But he looked at it as just because he was fuckin' around behind her back, it didn't mean that he was bad for her. He may be a bad boy, but Paris saw the good in Ace.

Standing out of bed, Ace pulled on his shorts. He exited the room and made his way into the kitchen with Paris, who was putting away the rest of the groceries. Ace took a seat on the countertop.

"Paris, I been thinkin' about our future and shit," Ace said sincerely.

Paris looked at him and replied, "Really? Well, you can't be about to propose to a bitch, because you're not on bended knee. So, what have you been thinking, baby?"

"Damn, dude," he chuckled. "Here a nigga is tryin' to be all sentimental and shit, and you can't help but throw shade. Anyway, like I was sayin', I wanna make sure you and Adonis are taken care of with or without me. So, I been thinking' about investin' in whatever you wanna do. I'll put in all of the cash, so all you gotta do is figure out whatever business you want and make it happen."

"For real, Ace?" She was gracious.

"Yeah. Bae, listen." He hopped down off the counter and stepped close to her. "You deserve for me to please you in any way I can. Look, I know your ass don't like when I'm in these streets, but this is why I do it, so we don't need for shit. And now, you can do whatever you want, all on me. Just name it."

"See, this is why I love your black ass so much, because you have always been a real nigga to me no matter what," Paris praised him. She wrapped her arms around his neck and kissed his lips. "Well, I do like my job at the daycare, but I rather have my own boutique. I already know what type of apparel that I want to sell and everything. All I need is a place to open one."

"Then start looking for a place and we'll make it happen. I'll use the lawyer me and Chedda have for our business and legal shit. He can help you get everything up and runnin'. All you gotta do is be a boss," Ace told her.

"Boy, I been a boss bitch," Paris half-joked. "But seriously. Thank you, bae."

"It ain't shit to a real boss," he jabbed at her, chuckling.

"Whatever, Ace!"

"Bae, I'm just fuckin' with you," Ace assured her. "Now come thank me with some more of that fire-ass head."

Ace smacked her ass as she started towards their bedroom. He took Adonis into his bedroom and lay him in his own bed. Then Ace made his way to his and Paris's bedroom, where she was awaiting him in bed ass naked.

Chapter 9

"Ace, get up. Ace? Get your black butt up, bae." Paris shook him awake. She had fucked him to sleep last night.

"I'm up, man, damn," Ace said as he rolled over facing her. "Whassup?"

"Thought you should know me and your son is about to leave out."

"A'ight." He stretched and yawned.

Paris sat on the edge of the bed. "Bae, I need some money."

"That's what you really woke a nigga up for? Just take the money on the nightstand."

"'Preciate it, bae." Paris grabbed the bundle of cash and placed it inside her Prada handbag. Before leaving with Adonis, she pecked Ace on the lips, then stood and said, "Have a good day."

Ace took a look at his iPhone and saw it was nearly eleven am. Also, he noticed there were some new texts and missed calls. Rolling out of bed in the nude, he stepped into the adjacent bathroom. First, he sat on the toilet and took a shit, then washed his hands afterwards. Next, he brushed his teeth, the bottom row was now bust-down with VVS diamonds and gold trim after getting them permanently placed in his mouth out in Texas. He had dropped twenty bands on his grill. Then, he jumped into the shower and washed off the sex from last night.

Subsequently, he got dripped out in a white, V-neck T-shirt, white Amiri jeans ripped on the knees with a Prada belt around his waist, and a pair of white Prada sneakers with the spikes. His jewelry consisted of a pair of diamond boogers in his ears, his gold Rolex with diamonds circling its face on his wrist, the bust-down Cuban link chain he had taken from

Forty's dead body was around his neck, and a pair of white and gold Cartier Buffalo frames with VVS diamonds embedded in the bridge of the frames sat propped on his face. He was looking like money, and money was his motive to kill.

Grabbing his keys and both iPhones off the nightstand, Ace pocketed them. In the closet near the front door, he collected his Glock and product before heading out the crib. He walked to the parking lot, then entered his Acura. Ace sat the switch on his lap, then he stashed the two Ziploc bags— filled with some eight-balls of crack and some seven grams sacks of loud pack—behind the driver's side door panel. He tossed back a Percocet tablet, then started the car and set off on his way.

While heading for the hood, Ace hoped to avoid twelve attempting to pull him over since he was ridin' dirty. He detoured to serve buyers hittin' his money-phone line for product along the way. Once Ace reached the hood, he pulled curbside and parked in front of Mika's house. His eight-year-old nephew, Breon, was riding his bike up and down the sidewalk, and Mika was sitting on the front porch steps, smoking a Newport cigarette and talking into her iPhone, while keeping a watchful eye on her son. Once Ace stepped outta the car, Breon braked his bike, then hopped off and hurried over to him.

"Hey, Uncle!" Breon said, excited to see him.

Ace was sure to hug him sideways so he wouldn't feel the bulge of the gun in his pocket. He said, "S'up, lil nigga."

"Where's Adonis? I wanna play with him."

"He's with his mama. I'll bring him over tomorrow."

"Okay."

"Listen, Abdul told me your bad ass tried stealin' from his store. Don't do that shit no more. Here." Ace fished out a sloppy bundle of money from his pocket and counted out a hundred bucks, then handed it to his nephew.

"Good lookin', Uncle!" Breon exclaimed.

"Now, go on and ride your bike." As Ace approached Mika, Breon went back to riding his bike. He sat on the steps beside his sister, who had ended her phone call. "That lil nigga looks just like his pops."

"Don't he," Mika concurred. "I just wish Tim could be here to see him."

"I know, right. Tim was a real-ass nigga, so I'm sure he would raise him right. Seems like most real niggas are either dead or in jail."

Mika cut her eyes at him. "If you know better, then you should do better, Ace."

Ace snorted. "Here you go with this shit again. Listen, I just came over to check on you, not to get lectured."

"I'm just sayin'. Look at what happened to Glen." She couldn't help but be reminded of her lil brother being murdered every day, with Gee's shrine still set up in front of her house.

"Sis, trust, you don't gotta remind me. I'ma take care of that shit."

"I just don't want you ending up in jail or dead behind that shit, Ace."

"Either way, it'll be worth it for lil bro. Mika, I 'preciate that you give a fuck and all, but this just the way it is."

Mika sighed. "Alright, bro. Long as you do know I give a fuck about your crazy ass. Look, I've found myself a place out in Green Bay, so I'll be moving outta these trenches soon."

"As much as I want you to move, it may sound dumb but, I feel my safest when I'm in the trenches."

"Well, not me. I need to be someplace where me and my baby don't have to worry about so many stray bullets and shit.

Plus, I'm tired of all these damn fiends and cops always in the area."

"I feel you. The goal is to get outta the hood without forgettin' where you came from," he told her. "But what about Granny's house? She left it to us, and we shouldn't abandon it."

"And we won't. When Mama gets out of jail, then she'll live here."

"I just hollered at her last night. Damn, I can't believe she finally about to come home in a few months. And I'ma make sure she don't need for nothin'."

"Ace, just try not to have her involved in your hustle."

"Mama's been a hustler, so she don't need me for that," Ace said. His iPhone chimed a text. He read the message and had to go and catch a play. "Sis, I gotta get to the money. I'll see you later."

"Okay, bro. Stay safe."

"I can't guarantee safety 'cause shit goes down, sis."

As Ace headed for his car he heard Mika yell at Breon not to ride his damn bike in the street. He entered the car then pulled off.

On the way to his destination, Ace rode with his switch in lap. He steered southbound on 27th Street. Ace yielded in the turning lane, awaiting traffic to pass in the intersection. He took the time to text his buyer that he would be there in a sec. While Ace waited to make a turn onto Nash Street, the silver Benz drew up beside him with Duke extending his arm out of the driver's window, aiming a handgun with an extended clip at the Acura.

Blam! Blam! Blam! Blam! Blam!

As a fusillade of bullets filled the Acura and shattered its tinted windows, Ace ducked his head then stabbed on the gas. He skirted into the intersection, then was T-boned by an oncoming vehicle, which caused the Acura to spin out of control and slam into a light pole. Duke zipped away from the scene in the Benz, hoping this time around he had killed Ace.

Once Ace collected himself, he grabbed his pipe, then forced the wrecked car door open and jumped out. Fortunately, he wasn't struck by the rapid gunfire or hurt badly in the collision. The only thing he suffered was a bruised ego. Hearing the blaring sirens vastly growing closer, Ace didn't even have time to grab his product from behind the door panel as he fled the scene afoot.

When Ace got a block away from the scene, he called Savvy to come pick him up at the Burger King he ducked inside of to lay low. So as not to look displaced, he ordered himself a meal from the breakfast menu, and then sat in a booth not eating while he waited. He was pissed just thinking about the product he had to leave in the car, it was worth at least ten G's.

Soon thereafter, Ace observed Savvy's Chrysler Sebring pulling into the parking lot, then he hurried outside to the car and stepped into the passenger's seat. Savvy knew something was up even though Ace didn't tell her much over the phone, because on her way she had passed the scene where his Acura was left shot up and crashed.

"Dude, what the fuck happened?" Savvy asked as she pulled out of the parking lot into traffic.

"Bitch-ass nigga who killed lil bro pulled up on me in traffic and shot up my Acura," Ace told her heatedly. He was heated as hell that Duke tried to down him. "On Gee, if I fuck around and catch dawg, I'ma blow his mu'fuckin' brains out!"

"Baby, calm down. What do you want me to do?"

"Take me to the storage so I can pick up my other whip."

Subsequent to picking up his red Infiniti G35, Ace zipped to Savvy's crib with her trailing. He jumped out of the whip then made his way into the house and went straight to his stash. Ace grabbed fifty G's, his Kevlar vest, and the Draco, he tossed it all on the bed. After pulling on the vest over his V-neck T-shirt, he stuffed the bundle of cash inside his jeans pocket, then grabbed up the Draco. On his way back outside, he introspectively stated, *I'ma show these hatin'-ass niggas how I'm comin'.*

Ace swaggered to his whip with the Draco in hand and hopped in the driver's seat. He honked the horn and waved Savvy over, who was sitting in her car talking on the phone. She stepped out and then walked over to the Infiniti.

"What's up, daddy?" Savvy asked, noticing he looked war ready.

"Record this shit on my live real quick," Ace instructed Savvy and handed her his iPhone. While Savvy recorded Ace on Facebook Live, Icewear Vezzo's track "First 48," played in the background. Ace pushed open the driver's door and had the Draco lying across his lap with the butt of the Glock and its extended clip hanging out of his jeans pocket. He spread out the fifty G's worth of crisp hundreds and spoke into the camera.

"Yeah, nigga, it's me! Hol' on, lemme turn this music down." Ace lowered the volume on the stereo just enough to talk over the music, then eyed the camera through his Cartier lenses. "First off, lemme say I wanted to keep away from all of this *Facebook* thuggin' shit. But I'ma say what I gotta say. For all you bitch-ass niggas that's wastin' bullets, sendin' shots and missin', who taught you bitch niggas how to shoot? All y'all did was fuck my whip up. I ain't trippin' 'cause it ain't no paper shortage over here. Still got G's on me, and I upgraded from the Acura to an Infiniti. Y'all best come correct whenever you see me and my niggas. 'Cause niggas armed and dangerous on my side. That's all I have to say. Now I'ma get back to the money. I'm finna really run it up on you bitch-ass broke boys!" Ace laughed into the camera.

Savvy ended the video, then asked, "Why you do that, Ace?"

"To show these niggas they ain't stoppin' shit. And I'ma keep shittin' on these hatin'-ass niggas every chance I get. Now gimme back my phone so I can slide," Ace told her and grabbed his phone.

Savvy just shook her damn head. "Anyway. You coming back tonight?"

"Yeah. But I'll be back late."

Savvy leaned into the car and gave him a peck on the lips before walking towards the house. Ace push-started the whip, then as he zipped off down the street his phone began to ring. He looked at the display and saw it was Paris.

"Whassup, baby?" Ace answered.

"I just saw your *Facebook Live*. You okay?" Paris asked, sounding concerned.

"Yeah, I'm good. Niggas shot up my whip." His tone was neutral. "Listen, I'ma be in the hood tonight so don't wait up."

"Really, dude? Niggas just tried to kill you, and your ass sitting here talking about not coming home to me and your son. You know what, Ace? Whatever," she said with an attitude.

"Don't gimme that attitude shit, Paris. I'll be home tomorrow."

"Tomorrow isn't guaranteed. Not with how you running the streets."

Ace nodded his understanding. "I know you concerned, but the streets ain't shit I can't handle. Look, just chill. I'ma call you later on."

After Ace ended the call with Paris, he phoned Chedda.

"What's poppin', my G?" Chedda answered.

"Nigga, while you all boo'd up with BM, my ass almost got smoked."

"Fuck you talkin' 'bout?"

"The nigga Duke caught me in traffic and turned my Acura into Swiss cheese."

"Dawg, where you at?"

"On my way to the hood. Just meet me there and I'll fill you in on shit."

"A'ight, fam. I'm on my way."

Once Ace made it to the hood, he parked the Infiniti at the curb in front of the trap spot. Ace sat the Draco in the passenger seat then stepped out of the car with the Glock in his pocket, clip protruding. Leaning back up against the whip, Ace watched the block. The block was hot, and not only because summertime was in full effect. Trappers and fiends were all around, and ratchet bitches and their hood babies were out about. Ace loved his hood and its people.

Soon thereafter, Chedda pulled up and parked his Audi behind the Infiniti. He stepped out with a TEC-9 hanging around his neck, wearing only a tank top, pajama pants, and Air Jordan sneakers. The two shook up, and then Ace filled Chedda in on what went down.

"Yeah, bro, we gotta put that nigga Duke, down," Chedda commented.

"That's on Gee," Ace vowed in agreement. His money-phone rang and he swiped "Ignore," because he didn't have any product with him. "You got some work with you right now?"

"Yeah."

"Grab your sack, and slide with me to catch some plays off my line real quick."

"A'ight."

Rich $avage 2

Ace jumped in his whip then grabbed the Draco out of the passenger seat and sat it on his lap. And Chedda went to his Audi, grabbed his product out the hidden compartment before entering the passenger side of the Infiniti.

"Damn, G, I see you got big Drac' on deck," Chedda pointed out, seeing the fully automatic.

Ace push-started the whip, and replied, "Just in case I catch any of Stone's pussy-ass niggas, I'ma nail they ass." He zipped away from the curb.

"Type shit." Chedda leaned back in his seat. "Niggas made you pull out the Infiniti on 'em, huh?" he grinned, displaying a mouth full of permanent teeth, now bust-down with the crushed diamonds and gold trim he had gotten done in Texas for thirty G's.

"Since they hit up my other car, had to pull out and show 'em it ain't shit. Just need to get a stash spot put in." Ace yielded as he approached a red light, then drove through once he saw the coast was clear. He was a bit 'noid after his whip was shot up earlier, so he perpetually watched every mirror for any signs of a tail.

"Take your shit to Shane's car shop, you know he'll hook you up with that."

"I'll do that ASAP. And I'ma have him throw some rims on my shit too, so I can really glaze on these broke boys," Ace boasted.

"Dawg, your ass a fool. I'ma pull out my new shit soon too," Chedda told him. "Speakin' of Shane though, we gon' have to get with him for some more work soon 'cause we about ran through the bricks he fronted us. On this re-up, I want us to cop ten blocks. That way we can be able to stack some cheese and still take care of our business and lawyer fees."

"I'm with that. But Shane gotta bless us with the price since we gon' cop that many birds at once," Ace laid out.

"I'll holla at him about it."

"Cool. Speakin' of business shit, I hollered at Paris about helpin' her start her owns. Said she wanna open a boutique, and I'ma help her. So I'ma need to have the lawyer take care of legal shit for her."

"A'ight. Good thing, you showin' love to your bitch like that, my nigga," Chedda complimented.

"Fa sho. I took heed to what you and me rapped about the other day. And you right, a nigga gotta make sure his main bitch know he gon' hold her down. Plus, Paris got my son and been down for my ass when I used to be flat broke and shit, so she deserves it. Don't get me wrong, Savvy's a good lil bitch but she ain't wifey material," Ace expounded.

"That's some one-hunnit shit. Listen, bro, we can't let shit get in our way of takin' care of business and family. That's why we can't let twelve or opps catch us slippin' in these streets, 'cause our people need us," Chedda expressed, offering his boy food for thought.

"I feel you on that shit, bro." Ace understood he needed to stay free and alive by any means.

Chapter 10

Ace pulled to the curb and braked Savvy's Chrysler in front of the Days Inn Hotel. He was bringing Savvy to a date with one of her tricks. Since his Infiniti was in the shop getting some work done to it, Ace was using Savvy's whip to bust moves for now.

"Boy, make sure your ass stay right here," Savvy insisted.

"I'll be waitin', so stop trippin'," Ace told her.

"Your ass better be."

"Sav, get the fuck out and go to your date."

Savvy grabbed her handbag that contained her condoms and baby Glock .9, both for her protection. She stepped out of the whip, and Ace admired her juicy ass jiggling in the leggings she wore as she strutted her way into the entrance of the hotel. While sitting in wait, Ace's iPhone rang. He grabbed up the phone and saw the call was from Sly.

"What's poppin', my nigga?" Ace answered.

"Pull up on me. I'm in the hood," Sly said.

"A'ight. I'll be there in like an hour."

"Cool."

Once Ace hung up, he replaced his phone in the cupholder. About twenty minutes later, Savvy came out of the hotel. She slipped back into the passenger seat of the car. Without words, Savvy handed over the cash to Ace that she had made from turning a trick. It wasn't a pimp and hoe situation, Ace and Savvy just supported each other's hustles in that way.

Looking in the side view mirror and seeing the street was clear, Ace pulled away from the curb. As he rode with his switch and sack in his lap on his way to bust moves, he listened to Peezy's tune, "There It Go." He took calls on his phone and zipped around the city, making serves. In between servin' yae and loud, he was accumulating a nice amount of cash. Though he was gettin' money hand over fist, Ace was determined to count up more money than he ever did. However, he knew he would have to get it how he live and was willing to do whatever it took.

After making a serve on the south side, Ace decided to make a pit stop at Shane's auto detailing shop that was located on that side of town. He wanted to check in on the progress of work done to his Infiniti thus far. He was having a couple of trap compartments installed inside his vehicle, which he would use for trafficking drugs. Therefore, whenever he was riding dirty, he wouldn't have to worry if twelve was to pull him over and search his car. Plus, he was having the twenty-four-inch chrome Forgiato rims, which he had stripped off Marco's whip, placed on the Infiniti.

Ace parked the Chrysler in front of Shane's shop. He instructed Sav to stay her ass in the car while he stepped out and entered the establishment. Knowing exactly who Ace was, a mechanic informed him the work on his car wouldn't be done until later. The mechanic took Ace to the car and showed him where the trap compartments were being installed, and Ace was satisfied with the placements. The rims hadn't been put on the car yet. Being that Shane wasn't there at the time, Ace decided to leave and would be sure to drop by later to pick up his whip.

Back in traffic, Ace steered to the north side of town. While stopped at the light on 35th and State Street, he got a call from Mika.

"What's Gucci, sis?" Ace answered.

"Bro, bring me some smoke," Mika told him.

"Damn, you ain't gon' even check on a nigga?"

Mika smacked her lips. "I know you good, boy."

"Big facts. I'll be there in a minute. Love you, sis."

"Love you, bro." Mika and Ace ended the call.

Once the traffic light turned green, Ace pulled off with traffic on his way to grab some more product after selling out. Making it to Savvy's crib, while Sav waited in the Chrysler, Ace went inside to his stash and grabbed a brick of white and an ounce of weed. Then he locked up the crib and hurried back to the car. Riding eastbound, Ace wove through traffic all the way to the hood. He turned onto his block, where he noticed Poppa and Bookie posted up on the sidewalk in front of the trap spot, servin' smokers. They had Beast-Mode with them.

Ace pulled the Chrysler near the curb across the street from the trap spot and parked. Ace peeped how Poppa and Bookie were observing the unfamiliar vehicle he was in, while clutching their poles. He pushed the driver's door open then stepped out, and the two relaxed seeing it was him.

"I see you two niggas were ready to bust," Ace pointed out as he stepped up over to Pop and Boo, who he shook up with.

"We ain't know who your ass was, pullin' up in that whip," Bookie said.

"That's my lil side-bitch whip." He rubbed Beast-Mode's head.

"Where your own shit at?" asked Poppa, in regard to Ace's car.

"Since my Acura got shot up, my other shit at the car shop gettin' some stash spots installed in it. A nigga gotta be able to ride with the stick in the box. Plus, I'm gettin' some rims thrown on that bitch," Ace answered.

"I feel you," Poppa replied.

Sly emerged from the trap spot. He and Ace stepped into the Chrysler to conduct business behind the tint, Ace in the driver's seat and Sly took up the backseat, since Sav was riding shotgun. Ever since Ace had encouraged Sly to get clean, Sly had been gettin' his sack right. And Ace liked seeing him do his thang.

"Here's the paper from the last front. It's ten racks," Sly informed as he handed over the stack of cash.

"A'ight." Ace handed the paper to Sav to put it with the rest, and now his bitch had a cool lil twenty G's in her purse. He reached beneath his seat and came up with a brick of cocaine and tossed it into Sly's lap. "I see you been doin' yo thang, and I believe you can handle that. Just bring me back thirty G's."

"I got you, my dude." Sly was on a paper chase.

The two shook up before Sly exited the whip with the brick in his pants. Ace honked the horn at his homies as he gunned away from the curb.

"Daddy, that nigga ain't right," Savvy pointed out. She peeped how Sly eyed her, and it made her uncomfortable.

"What makes you say some shit like that about my nigga?" Ace wanted to know.

"I'ont know, it's just something about him that rubbed me wrong. Call it a woman's intuition."

"It ain't like that with Sly."

"Well, just make sure you watch his ass."

"I hear you, boo." Ace thought she was trippin', but he would keep it in mind. He drove around the corner to Mika's house. Ace asked Savvy to come inside with him, and she did so.

"Hey, bro," Mika greeted.

"S'up, big sis." Ace offered her a hug.

"Who's your friend?" she asked about the girl with him.

"This is my lil bitch, Savvy. Savvy, this my sis, Mika." he introduced them.

"Girl, I'ont know what you see in my crazy-ass lil brotha," Mika half-joked.

"I know, right!" Savvy chuckled, jokingly. "But he's a good nigga."

"If you say so." Mika thought Savvy was cool, but she was like sisters with Paris.

"On some other shit," Ace piped in, changing the subject. He handed Mika a bag of the cookie weed. "That's on love. Look, I gotta go and catch plays. Call me if you need me."

Ace, along with Savvy, was now on his way to get to the bag. Needing some petrol after commuting through town, Ace pulled into the gas station located in his hood and parked at a gas pump. He directed Savvy's ass to go and purchase thirty bucks' worth of gas and a box of Swisher Sweets blunts. Sav stepped out of the car and went inside to do as told. While Ace sat inside the car behind the tinted windows, he kept his hand on the stick in his lap, just in case a nigga got the idea to try him.

Ace's phone chimed, indicating he received a text message. He saw the text was from Shane and read it.

SHANE:

Your ride is ready for pick up.

Ace couldn't wait to see how his shit looked with the rims now on it. He replied via text.

ACE:

On the way.

Looking through the rearview mirror, Ace noticed the familiar chameleon-painted Cadillac CTS on chrome rims enter the lot, which pulled up and braked beside the Chrysler. Ace knew the 'Lac belonged to the pimp nigga, Toucan. Its passenger window dashed down, and there was Toucan with his neck and wrist iced out. He gestured for the window to be rolled down, expecting to find Savvy, but to Toucan's dismay, when the window dashed down, the driver of the Chrysler was Ace.

"Whuddup?" Ace said assertively while mean-muggin'.

"Oh. Thought you was Savvy. My bad, pimp," Toucan uttered, looking thrown. He didn't know Ace personally, but he had seen him a couple times at the strip club where Savvy worked with a few of his hoes. Now he realized Savvy apparently belonged to Ace.

"No problem. But for the record, I'ma savage, not a pimp."

"Whatever is clever," Toucan replied. "Listen, I'ont know if Savvy is your girl or what, but she's a keeper. Treat a girl good and she'll treat you better. That's just a lil game for you."

Ace could tell Toucan was fishing for answers, so he dryly remarked, "Type shit."

Stepping out the whip with his switch in hand, Ace then stuffed the gun in the front pocket of his Off-White jeans, in Toucan's sight. As Ace turned to pump the gas, Toucan pulled off. A moment later, Savvy returned to the car. After pumping the gas, Ace slid back behind the steering wheel.

"I seen you talkin' to Toucan. What was that about?" Savvy inquired.

Ace glanced over at her. "That nigga pulled up, thinkin' it was you in the car. Talkin' 'bout you're a keeper, like he tryin' to pull you. You need to tell dawg clown-ass to fall back."

"Ace, I already told him that. So, he knows," Savvy reassured.

"Did you holla at dawg about havin' some of his hoes work at our club yet?"

"Not yet. But I will, soon as you and Chedda ready to hold auditions for the girls."

"That shouldn't be long from now."

"And Nina told me y'all talked about her working there too."

"We did." Ace wondered if Nina had also told her they talked about how Nina wanted to fuck him. But he kept that to himself for now. "She's your bestie, so I figured you'd be cool with it."

"Yeah, I'm cool with her working there," Sav told him. "Gimme some smoke so I can roll up real quick." She took a blunt out of the box, and Ace passed her a sack of the cookie weed.

When Ace was finna pull out of the lot into traffic, he noticed the unmarked Dodge Magnum that belonged to the dirty cops, Lucas and Bradshaw. Ace was well aware Lucas was determined to nab him for questioning on a couple of homicides that had occurred around the hood. But Ace wasn't willing to go back to prison.

"Sav, hold my shit, 'cause I'm 'bout ta dip on twelve," Ace told her as he passed her his sack of product and gun.

"You fuckin' serious right now?" Savvy asked rhetorically.

"Don't ask questions, just do as I say. And if we get jammed, then your ass best not say shit to twelve."

Savvy smacked her lips. "Ace, I already know that shit."

"You better."

Once the Magnum's sirens blared, Ace gunned out of the lot, cutting off oncoming traffic in his attempt to flee. He peeped in the rearview mirror and saw the Magnum in high pursuit. Ace dipped around a city bus and turned a sharp corner, but still wasn't able to shake the Magnum on his tail. Lucas collided the Magnum into the side of the Chrysler in an attempt to halt Ace.

Heading towards a red light with traffic passing across caused Lucas to yield the Magnum, yet Ace zipped through the red light, narrowly avoiding a collision as motorists honked their horns in protest. Though it was a reckless move on Ace's part, it had gotten him away from Lucas, who was stuck waiting on traffic to clear. Ace bent several corners and was finally convinced that he had shaken the dirty cops. He went on his way.

"Ace, them bitches fucked up my damn car, dude!" Savvy cried out heatedly over the wreckage done to her car from the collision. "And my insurance won't even cover the costs."

"Baby, don't even trip. I'ma get the car fixed for you," Ace assured her.

Savvy leaned back in her seat with her arms folded and pouted. "It better be good as fuckin' new, too, Ace." She muffed Ace's head when he laughed at her. "Ain't shit funny, boy. I'm serious as hell!"

"Why you actin' like you mad and shit? Said I'ma get it fixed, damn," Ace remarked.

"Your ass better."

Ace headed back to Shane's auto detailing shop to pick up his Infiniti. He pulled the Chrysler inside the garage port, where his car was awaiting him. The trap compartments were installed, and the rims had been put on. Ace approved of the work done to his whip. By now Shane was there and came from the back office to mingle with Ace.

"How you, homes?" Shane greeted him.

"I'm good," Ace replied.

"Hope you're satisfied with the work my boys did on your whip."

"Yeah, I needed a stash in my shit. And the rims look beasty on this bitch!" he approved. "Now I need your boys to fix up my lil bitch car."

"What all do you want done to it, besides the obvious?" Shane noticed the damage on the driver's side, the door was badly dented, side view mirror was missing and the headlight was dangling.

"Fix all the damage, then give it a paint job. Savvy, what color do you want the car painted?"

Savvy thought on it a moment. "Um, paint it money green."

"Done," Shane said. "Don't worry, Ace, my boys will have it all done in a few days, and it won't cost you much."

Ace pulled out his bankroll, then counted out seventy-five-hundred dollars and handed it to Shane. "That should cover costs. Look, I gotta bounce."

"Homes, I'll see you and Chedda soon enough for a re-up."

"Fa sho."

Ace, along with Savvy, entered his Infiniti. They jumped back in traffic, leaving behind Savvy's Chrysler to be repaired and painted. This time around, Savvy was pushing the whip while Ace rode shotgun. He answered his phone and directed her where to go in order to make his serves.

After dumpin' his whole sack, he instructed her to go to the crib. Parking the Infiniti in front of her place, Savvy peered over at Ace, who was oblivious to her eyes on him while he focused on counting up profits. She loved the shit out of this nigga. She thought, *his black ass know he's sexy.*

Ace looked up and peeped her eyes on him. "I see you lookin' with your lookin'-ass," he said with a smile, the VVS diamonds dancing in the lower row of his teeth.

"I love when you smile, it makes me wet," Savvy purred.

"You know I'm the shit. I'm doin' what your last nigga could never do."

"Ace, I'ont care nothing about your status. I'm your ride or die, so it's whatever. Because you make me better."

"Listen, I respect that you more realer than these niggas, and you ain't with no extra shit 'cause you about your cheese."

She eyed him through slits. "Do you love me?"

"Shit, I think I do," he told her.

"I know you're caught in between me and Paris. And I don't wanna fight her over you...instead, I would rather hang with her. Because I'm with whatever you're with. So, if you see another bitch you like, then I'll go get her. Why creep on me when we can just fuck her together? I know my place, Ace, so I ain't worried about no other bitch taking my spot," Sav expressed.

Ace had to admit he did love his lil bitch. "Good to know your ass understand I'm in charge. Keep it that way," he responded coolly. "Now, let's go in the crib so I can stash these racks."

"Sounds good to me, Zaddy."

Once they were in the crib, Ace made Sav roll up a blunt of cookie weed, while he counted up the profits from the day. They were seated on the couch in the front room. The money came out to twenty-six racks.

"Daddy, you be gettin' paid!" Sav praised his grind.

"It ain't shit to a nigga." Ace handed her his iPhone, and said, "Take some pics of me real quick."

"Boy, your ass stay flexin'."

Savvy took a few pictures of Ace flexed up with them racks in hand, while he was dripped in diamonds and gold, with his .45 Glock lying across his lap. He posted the pictures on his *Facebook* and captioned it: #RICH $AVAGE.

Chapter 11

While Paris was still getting dressed, Ace was already dressed for their double date tonight with Chedda and his girl, Antoinette. He rocked an Amiri denim jeans and jacket outfit, with a Christian Louboutin T-shirt, belt, and sneakers. Plus, he was drippin' in jewels.

It was Paris and Antoinette's plan to go out with their men on a double date, Ace and Chedda didn't have much of a choice but to go along with it. And there wouldn't be any kids along with them, so Mika was to watch Adonis for the night. Besides, Ace could use a night out with his girl, away from the streets.

Ace peeped at his Rolly and saw it was 8:15 pm. He was in the bedroom, seated on the edge of the bed, impatiently waiting on Paris' ass to finish getting ready when his iPhone chimed. He looked at the display and noticed there was a text message from Kiki and read it.

KIKI:

I need to see you.

Ace knew that she was referring to a re-up on work. He sent a text in reply.

ACE:

Cool. I'ma pull up on you in a min.

After sending the text, Ace made his way into the bathroom and found Paris applying her make-up. "Damn, bae. Your ass still in here gettin' ready?"

"Boy, you can't rush a bad bitch," Paris replied.

"Hope you don't take this wrong, but when you be just chillin' with no make-up on, that's when you're the baddest. Look, I'm finna just go ahead and drop off Adonis at my sister's place. Then you should be ready by the time I get back." This was his way of doing two things at the same damn time, while giving Paris some time to get ready.

Paris stopped what she was doing, then eyed him, and insisted, "You better come straight back too, Ace." She returned to beating her face.

"A'ight," Ace assured her. "I'ma take your whip."

"Alright."

Ace pecked her on the cheek before leaving her to finish up and going to collect his son. He grabbed his product and .45 Glock out of the closet near the front door and pocketed it before he and Adonis left out. Outside, Ace noticed the night was just about to fall due to the sun's setting. He sat his son in the car seat before making his way around to enter the driver's side of Paris's Honda Accord. As Ace slid behind the wheel, he thought, *I gotta upgrade my bitch car.*

Ace placed his pole and sack beneath the seat. Once he started the Accord, Lakeyah's tune "Too Much," commenced playing. He flicked on the headlights, then pulled out of the parking lot on his way to the hood.

"Where us goin', Daddy?" Adonis asked.

"I'm takin' you to Auntie Mika house, so you can play with Breon," Ace told him.

"Okay."

"And you better be good, or I'ma whoop your ass."

"Mommy don't whoop me."

"But Daddy do," Ace replied as he braked at a stoplight on Fond du Lac Avenue. "And I only do it 'cause I'ont want you doin' nothin' you ain't s'pose to be doin'. I'ont want you makin' none of the same bad choices I happened to make while growin' up. I just want for you to become a better man than me. 'Cause Daddy luh you, boy." He loved being a dad to his son, and he didn't want Adonis to lose him the same way he lost his own pops. However, Ace was knee deep in the streets, so he couldn't promise he wouldn't go out like his own pops did. But for as long as Ace lived, he would be there for his son.

"Me love you too, Daddy. And me not gon' be bad," Adonis promised.

"Good."

Once the light flipped green, Ace pulled off with traffic headed eastbound. Arriving in the hood, he turned onto the block then pulled to the curb and parked across the street from Mika's place. Reaching beneath the driver's seat, he came up with the Glock and placed it on his waist before stepping out of the car and grabbing Adonis out of his car seat. They made their way into the house.

After dropping off his son with Mika, Ace made his way back outside to the car and offered Reverend Johnson a wave as he jumped into the driver's seat of the Accord. He dipped around the corner to serve Kiki. He texted her that he was outside, a moment later, she emerged from the duplex house then entered the passenger seat.

"Hey, big bro," Kiki greeted.

"S'up," Ace replied.

"I see you drippin' and shit. What're you all dressed up for?"

"Me and Paris finna go out with Don and Antoinette tonight. Her ass at the crib still gettin' ready."

"Y'all have fun."

"I'm sure we will. Anyway, I brought the work for you." He came up from under the seat with four and a half ounces of crack, then handed it to her. "It's a four and a split."

Kiki put the dope in her Louis handbag, then dug out a sloppy bundle of money, passed it to him and assured, "That's all of the money." She was good at trappin' and Ace liked that about her. "Bro, you got some weed?"

"Yeah. Roll this up real quick."

Ace gave her a sack of loud and Kiki grabbed a blunt out of the cupholder to roll up. While the two sat in the parked car smoking the weed, they reminisced about Gee. Both of them missed Glen so much. Though he was gone, he wasn't forgotten.

"What about the time when lil bro fool-ass paid that smoker some crack to light himself on fire?" Ace remembered.

"That smoker was running around screaming like crazy! But the funniest part was when his ass stopped, dropped, and rolled!" Kiki mentioned, then she and Ace busted out laughing.

Ace hit the weed and then passed it to her. "Damn, I miss the shit outta Gee."

"Me too. He was my baby. I'ont think I'll ever meet another nigga like him." Kiki inhaled some weed smoke.

"Just make sure you take your time to get over lil bro," Ace advised. His phone chimed and it was a text message from Paris.

PARIS:
Where u at? I been ready.

Ace didn't realize that he had been gone longer than expected. He replied via text.

ACE:
Now yo' ass knows how it feel
to have someone waitin'. OTW.
PARIS:
Boy, just hurry up.

Ace replaced the phone in the cupholder. "Look, I gotta get back to Paris. Hit me up if you need me for anything."

"Okay, bro. Tell Paris I said hey."

Once Kiki exited the car, Ace pulled away from the curb on his way to the crib to scoop up Paris. Soon thereafter, he arrived at their complex and parked in front. Following sending Paris a text, she met him outside.

Ace thought she was looking good with her hair in a half-up half-down style. Paris was wearing some form-fitting jeans cut on the thighs, with a halter top. Fortunately for her, her titties didn't sag or flop all over the place, so she could go braless. A pair of Christian Louboutin stilettos and matching clutch purse completed her outfit. Her accessories were diamond hoop earrings and a tennis bracelet.

They approached the Infiniti, Ace held open the passenger's door for Paris before he entered the driver's side. He placed the pistol beneath his seat. They set off on their way to meet up with the others at Benihana's.

"What took you so long getting back, Ace?" Paris questioned him.

"After I dropped off our son, I had to make a stop to see Kiki. And she said hey," Ace let her know.

"Oh, okay."

Ace glanced over at her, shaking his damn head. "What, you don't trust a nigga?"

"I trust you enough. But I ain't a fool either. I see how all of them little girls be all on your dick on *Facebook* and shit, like they don't even care about the pics of us together that's posted on your page. Them bitches don't got shit on me."

"Paris, I'ont give two fucks about no *Facebook* friends or beef. Who means everything to me?"

"I do," she answered in a lowered voice.

"Right. And you the one who a nigga with," Ace expressed. Although he was fuckin' Savvy, he was cuffin' Paris.

"I hear you."

Martell "Troublesome" Bolden

Once making it to Benihana's, Ace and Paris made their way into the restaurant. They found the table that was occupied by Chedda and Antoinette, then Ace and Chedda shook up while Paris and Antoinette hugged, before they all took their seats. Shortly thereafter, a waiter approached the table, and the foursome made their orders. As they awaited their dinner, Ace and Chedda talked about investing their money in other areas, while Paris and Nett chatted about their relationships, work, and children. The double date was going well.

Chedda turned to Antoinette, and said, "Baby, I'm finna hit up the restroom real quick."

"M'kay. Hurry back," Nett cooed, then pecked Chedda's lips before he stood and headed for the restroom. She turned her attention to Ace and said, "So, Ace. When do you plan on putting a ring on my girl's finger?"

"Nett, girl, would you stop?" Paris chimed in. She already knew how Ace felt about getting married, even though she wouldn't mind it. "Ace, you don't have to answer that."

Ace leaned back in his seat. "Listen, Nett, no matter how expensive a ring is, it will never amount to how much a nigga feel for Paris," he replied to Antoinette's question. After his boy, Chedda, had recently popped the question to Nett, Ace knew she just wanted him to do the same for Paris.

"Just don't do my girl wrong, Ace," Nett responded.

Soon after Chedda returned to the table and took his seat with the others, their orders were delivered. They held conversation over dinner and drinks. After enjoying their meals and each other's company for the night, the couples said their parting words before they parted ways.

Subsequent to picking up their son, Ace pushed the car headed home while Paris sat back in the passenger's seat and Adonis laid on the back seat asleep. During the commute, Ace

102

checked the rearview mirror more so out of habit, and he noticed a suspect vehicle a few lengths behind that seemed to be tailing them. He didn't care to alarm Paris, so he didn't mention it, but he discreetly reached beneath the seat, then came up with his Glock and held it in his lap. As Ace approached a red light on 35th and Villard Street, he yielded the car to a halt. He gripped the Glock, ready to air out the suspect vehicle, but it shifted into the turning lane and bent a right at the corner going the other way.

Damn, all this beef in these streets got a nigga on edge, Ace mused with a sigh of relief as he replaced his gun beneath the seat. He was relieved his girl and son weren't in harm's way due to his beefs. All he wanted to do was protect them and provide for them. Ace glanced into the back seat at his sleeping son, then over to his girl, and he realized how much they meant to him.

Once the light turned green, Ace pulled off headed home. He knew never to bring beef to where he and his lay their heads.

Martell "Troublesome" Bolden

Chapter 12

In the hood, Ace pulled to the curb in front of the trap spot and parked. There were so many foreign whips parked on the block that it looked like a dealership, and all of them were owned. Along with Ace's red Infiniti G35, there was Chedda's black Benz Jeep, Poppa's white Lexus IS, Bookie's yellow Audi Quattro, and Sly's silver Jaguar SUV. Each of the vehicles were a symbol of their riches.

Ace pocketed his pole before pushing the driver's door open and departing the car. Once he entered the spot, he found the gang in the kitchen. Along with a Draco and two Glocks with extended clips on them, there was a money-counter and bundles of cash set out on the table, all profit from the last load. And Ace had come to collect his payout. His whole gang had come up, and now money wasn't a thang. Of them all, Ace had the biggest bank. But he and his niggas were all on, so now when bitches saw them, they couldn't tell who's the richest.

"I see you niggas ain't wastin' no time gettin' to the money," Ace said.

"Time is money," Chedda commented while seated at the table. He nodded at a large stack of cash. "That's all you, right there."

Ace grabbed the cash and thumbed through it. "That's what money do!"

"Broke niggas don't know shit about that," Bookie laughed, who was seated at the table also. He was pouring up a bottle of dirty Sprite.

"Let's hit the club tonight and hurt some broke-ass niggas' feelings," Poppa suggested while he stood off to the side, counting out a handful of cash.

"I ain't really feelin' like hittin' no clubs. So, I'm good on that," Ace said.

"I'm good on the club tonight, too. Got some other shit planned," Chedda chimed in.

"I'm with it. What about you, Sly?" Bookie wanted to know.

Sly stood at the stove, cooking up some work. "Fuck the club, I rather get this paper," he answered.

"Look, I'm finna bounce. I'll get up with y'all niggas." Ace shook up with the gang before making his way out the spot. It was growing dark outside, so Ace was on the lookout for jack-boys, because with all the bread he had on him, he was a walking lick. When he jumped inside the whip, he turned on the headlights and dispelled away from the curb. Ace was on his way to drop off the money with the rest of his stash at Savvy's crib. He dipped through traffic while listening to Icewear Vezzo's tune, "Free B. Allen."

Arriving at his destination, Ace spun the block thrice before he decided no one had tailed him and then parked behind Savvy's good-as-new Chrysler Sebring. He stepped out and made his way into the crib. Upon entering, Ace found Savvy in the front room seated on the couch beside Nina. The two were sharing a blunt while talking about some leakin'-ass nigga that always showed up at the club they worked, trying to short-change them.

"Since you bitches don't got shit else better to do, go ahead and count up this paper for me," Ace butted in. He pulled the cash out and tossed the bundles on the coffee table positioned in front of them.

"Damn, all that money!" Nina cooed, seeing the thick bundles of cash wrapped with rubber bands.

"Okay, daddy. We got you," Savvy assured him.

"When y'all done, let me know how much it is. I'm finna go and hop in the shower."

Leaving the bitches to count his bread, Ace headed to the bedroom, where there was an adjacent bathroom. He hooked up his two iPhones onto the chargers before placing them on the nightstand, along with his .45 Glock. Then he removed his Cartier frames, Cuban link chain, and Rolly watch, placing them on the nightstand also. Once Ace stepped into the bathroom, he turned on the hot water and let it heat up whilst taking off his designer clothes. After gathering his shower essentials, he got in the shower and hot water cascaded on him.

Following his lengthy shower, Ace dried himself off. He wrapped a dry towel around his waist and padded barefoot into the adjacent bedroom. Once entering the room, Ace came upon Savvy and Nina, who were both ass naked, lying in the king-sized bed, blanketed with all of the money.

"Just so you know how much money is here, sixty racks," Savvy let him know.

"And this much money makes bitches' pussies wet," Nina added.

"Y'all know it's money over bitches, right?" Ace half-joked, grinning.

"How 'bout you have both?" Savvy responded.

"Now, c'mere," Nina said, and coaxed him over with her manicured index finger.

Ace allowed the towel to fall onto the floor as he slid into bed between the girls. Savvy began kissing him, then she reached over grabbing Nina by the back of her head and pulled her in for a three-way kiss. Leaning back, Ace allowed the girls to kiss while he watched. He could tell it wasn't the first time for Savvy and Nina.

Nina grabbed Savvy's hand, pulled her out of bed, and now they stood before Ace. Seductively, Nina slow rolled her hips and twerked her ass back against Savvy's crotch. Savvy reached around and played with Nina's pretty titties and slipped a finger in her pussy. Both girls got down on the floor, positioning themselves on all fours, side by side, and began bouncing their asses. While the girls put on a private show for Ace, he grabbed a fistful of the bills from the bed and made it rain on them.

Both of the girls seductively crawled over to Ace. Savvy grabbed his hard dick in her petite, manicured hand and began stroking it and Nina fondled his nut sack. Both the bad bitches licked the tip of his dick at the same damn time, their tongues interacting. Ace pulled Nina up and into the money blanketed bed. While he lay back, she straddled his face, and he ate her pussy. Savvy took it upon herself to climb onto his lap and slide her pussy down on the dick, she rode him reverse cowgirl. Each of the girl's moans of pleasure bounced off the walls. Ace spread Nina's pussy lips and slipped two fingers deep inside her twat and played with her clit. She tossed her head back as he orally pleasured her. All the while, Savvy slammed her snug twat up and down on his piece.

"Mmmm... I'm cummmin!" Savvy groaned. "Damn, nigga... This dick so fuckin' good!" Her pussy juices oozed as the tip of his dick hit her G-spot.

"Now I want you to eat her pussy while I fuck you from the back," Ace told Nina.

"'Kay, boo," Nina purred, all for it.

Laying back in bed, Savvy spread her legs wide, and while on her hands and knees, Nina lowered her luscious lips onto Savvy's wetness. She flicked her tongue over Savvy's clit as she finger-fucked her wet-ass pussy, and Savvy moaned and played with her own hard nipples. Ace positioned himself behind Nina and slid his pole deep inside her walls. He dug her out, causing Nina to arch her back deeply while taking the full length of his dick. While fuckin' her from behind, Ace smacked her ass, and Nina threw her pussy back as she creamed on his big dick.

She was turned on so damn much, she licked and sucked on Savvy's pussy vigorously, slurping up her cum juices. And Savvy was in a trance as she grasped the back of Nina's head, pressing Nina's mouth onto her twat. All the while, Savvy and Ace gazed into each other's eyes as they both were being pleasured by Nina. The bitch was excellent at eating pussy, and she could take some dick!

Feeling a nut swell up in the tip of his dick, Ace pulled out of Nina's pussy and squirted warm semen all over her phat ass. Ace sank back into the pillow as the girls lay on either side of him. He kissed them both, and yawned, "No lie, y'all two bitches did your thang! That shit was what a nigga needed."

It wasn't long before Ace and the girls had fallen asleep on the bed blanketed with money. His street dreams of getting rich were turning into reality. He had gotten his money and weight up in a major way for nearly a year, since he had been home from prison. Although, instead of time, the only thing he seemed to keep track of was his profits and product.

Thus far, Ace's entire stash amounted to three hundred and seventy-eight G's, on top of working with four bricks of yae and twelve pounds of weed. Plus, he had upwards to a hundred G's worth of jewelry sitting on the nightstand. Also, he owned his Infiniti G35, embellished with twenty-four-inch chrome Forgiato rims. Not to mention, he possessed a Draco, AR-15, twin .45 Glocks with thirty-two-shot sticks, and a Kevlar vest in his personal arsenal. Even still, Ace was out to get richer than ever the savage way.

***

Hearing the buzz of his iPhone awakened Ace. He'd been in a sex-induced slumber after slayin' Savvy and Nina. The digital clock glowing next to his two phones on the nightstand told him it was nearly two in the morning.

Fuck callin' me this damn late? Ace wondered. He reached over Nina, grabbed the phone, then checked its display and saw the *FaceTime* call was from Poppa. Ace figured that somethin' had to be up. While lying in bed between Savvy and Nina, he took the call.

"Whassup, lil bro?" Ace answered. On his phone screen he saw that Poppa and Bookie were in the car, and he could hear Lil Durk's tune "When We Shoot," playing in their background.

"On Gee, we just caught that bitch-nigga Duke and dropped his ass!" Poppa told him, geeked up off the kill.

"How the fuck y'all manage to do that?"

"While we was in the club, I seen dawg when he came in with his niggas. So, me and bro crept out the club and waited on the stupid-ass niggas in the parking lot," Poppa informed. He turned the camera on Bookie, who was driving, as he piped in.

"And once the pussy-ass niggas stepped foot in the parking lot, we aired 'em out. Them niggas took off runnin', so me and bro chased Duke down," Bookie input.

Poppa returned the camera onto himself, now flashing a Glock with a thirty-shot stick. "Big bro, you know how the fuck we slidin', pop out with the ratchet and then shit get tragic!" He laughed.

"Y'all got some get-back for Gee, I tilt my hat," Ace commended them. "But I still want that hoe-ass nigga, Stone.

His ass gon' be sick with it when he finds out he lost his dawg. Did anybody see y'all down the nigga?"

"Besides them scary-ass niggas that left him for dead, I'ont think so," Poppa answered.

"A'ight. Don't slide then post it on *Facebook*," Ace advised.

Bookie chimed in, "That shit lame to us."

"Facts," Poppa cosigned. He peeped that Ace was sandwiched between two bad bitches. Both the girls had stirred awake, Savvy lay with her head on Ace's shoulder and Nina waved into the camera. "Now I see why you didn't wanna hit up the club with us. I see you got a coupla baddies in a bed full of money!"

"Rich savage shit." Ace smirked.

"Type shit."

"Listen, y'all niggas stay low. I'ma get with y'all later. Plenty much love." After ending the call, Ace replaced his phone on the nightstand.

Too overcome with different emotions in the moment, Ace couldn't go back to sleep. Hearing that Pop and Boo had whacked Duke was some vindication, but who he really wanted dead was Stone. Although Ace had gained more love for Poppa and Bookie for going hard on the strength of Glen. He introspectively said, *on Gee, I'ma kill that bitch-ass nigga, Stone.*

"Everything alright, daddy?" Sav asked as she rubbed his bare chest.

"Yeah, it ain't shit," Ace told her. "Just lil bro n'em lit as fuck after leavin' the club."

Nina slid her hand down to his dick, and said, "Forget about that shit, boo. Let a bitch get some more of this big dick."

Ace lay back while he watched the girls take turns sucking his dick. He didn't mind fuckin' two bad bitches at the same damn time.

Chapter 13

Ace pulled his Infiniti curbside and parked across the street from the trap spot. Chedda, Poppa and Bookie, along with some others, posted in front of the trap while Sly was inside. Chedda was standing, leaned back up against his Benz with his back towards the street, talking into his iPhone. Poppa sat on the porch steps, counting some paper he had just gained from a smoker. And Bookie was standing on the sidewalk, spittin' game at a bitch from around the hood. Being that it was summertime, the hood was live. Kids were playing outside while parents watched over them.

After Ace took a puff from the blunt of loud, he was finna open the driver's door to step out. His iPhone chimed, indicating he had received a text-message. Looking at the display, Ace saw the text was from Paris. He remained seated in the whip while he read the message.

PARIS:
Stop by Walmart and pick up
some Pull-Ups for Adonis.

"Damn, I just brought some Pull-Ups 'bout a week ago for his lil shitty ass," Ace muttered to himself as he exhaled a thick cloud of weed smoke from his nostrils. Even though Ace ran the streets, he always did his part to take care of home. Paris and his son were one of the main reasons he put his life on the line so he could make sure they didn't need for shit. He replied to Paris via text.

ACE:
A'ight. Just gimme about an hour
and I'll be on my way there.
PARIS:
Ace, don't have me and your son
waiting on your ass for too long.

ACE:
Bae, I'ma be there once I get done
bustin' moves.
PARIS:
Kay.
Ace sat the phone on his lap alongside the Glock. He hit the blunt once more before placing it in the ashtray. While sitting in the parked car, through his side view mirror, Ace peeped a blue Chevy Malibu crawling down the block. Before he could register what the hell was going down, niggas suddenly popped out of the front and back passenger side windows, hanging halfway out the Malibu, gripping fully-automatics and bustin' at everyone posted in front of the trap.

Prraat! Prraat! Prraat!

Rrraa! Rrraa!

Once the automatic gunfire erupted, Ace ducked out of instinct. Apparently, the shooters hadn't noticed him sitting in the car. He immediately grabbed the switch from his lap, opened his driver door ajar, then stuck the barrel out and dumped numerous slugs into the driver's side of the Malibu.

Boc! Boc! Boc! Boc! Boc! Boc!

Skiiirrrt!

As bullets from Ace's Glock filled the Malibu, the car skirted off down the street.

Poppa came out the gangway with a Draco, airin' out the car until it made a sharp turn at the corner. Ace pushed his door completely open and jumped out of the car with his pole in hand. He noticed Bookie tending to Chedda, who was lying on the sidewalk, bleeding profusely from catching a slug in his stomach. And Bookie had gotten hit in his forearm. Although Chedda was still breathing, he was gasping for air, while Bookie was on his knees applying pressure to Chedda's bullet wound, in the hopes of slowing down the blood flow.

Rushing out from the trap with a TEC-9 in hand, Sly found the block in a frenzy.

"It's gon' be okay, Chedda, just soldier through this shit," Bookie encouraged.

"Help me carry bro," Ace directed Poppa, and they hurried over to Chedda.

"Take him to my whip," Sly instructed as Poppa and Ace lifted Chedda up off the ground.

Bookie ran across the street to Sly's Jag truck parked curbside and pulled open its back door as Ace and Bookie carried Chedda towards the SUV. As they loaded Chedda into the back seat, Sly slid behind the wheel and Bookie jumped into the passenger side, they both held their guns in hand just in case the shooters decided to spin the block once more. Ace and Poppa sat in back with Chedda, his head lay in Ace's lap and his Air Jordan sneakers were in Poppa's, who continued to apply pressure to Chedda's bullet wound. Sly peeled off down the street, headed to the nearest hospital in a rush.

So much shit ran through Ace's mind as they raced through traffic. He couldn't help but think back to when he had first met Chedda. Ever since then, they had been through it all together. They had slept in the same bed, wore the same clothes, busted at the same opps, and even fucked some of the same hoes. They had been through a lot of shit and managed to survive. And Ace hoped his boy would survive this time also. He had already lost Gee, and he didn't want to lose any more of his bros.

"Chedda, look at me. Stay with us," Poppa insisted.

"I-I'm...I'm not...d-dyin' like th-this," Chedda managed to utter through ragged breaths. He was in excruciating pain.

Ace looked into his eyes and stated, "Your ass bet not die on us, Chedda. Don't give them bitch-ass niggas what they want."

"Who the fuck were those niggas anyway?" Sly wanted to know. He zoomed through a red light.

"Them were the same bitch-niggas who ran off and left Duke the night we dropped his ass," Bookie said. He grunted as he nursed his wounded arm.

"You good, Boo?" Ace asked out of concern.

"Shit burns like hell, but it's nothin'. I just hope Chedda gon' be a'ight," he responded.

"Soon as we get bro to the hospital, he should be all good," Ace said, hopefully.

Chedda coughed up some blood. He was fading in and out of consciousness.

"Faster, Sly!" Poppa implored. He didn't want Chedda to die before they could get him some help to possibly save his life.

"Goin' as fast as I can," Sly replied. He blared the horn at the vehicles ahead in traffic out of frustration as he swerved around it. "We're almost at the hospital, so don't trip."

"Just hold on, my nigga!" Ace urged Chedda.

Arriving at Froedtert Hospital, Sly pulled to the ER entrance. While Sly remained in the SUV, Ace immediately jumped out the car, then assisted Poppa with hauling Chedda inside the ER. Bookie demanded the nurses' help. Two nurses rolled over a stretcher, then Ace and Poppa placed Chedda on it before the nurses rushed him away to the operation room. Also, Bookie was taken for medical attention on his wounded arm.

Ace looked to Poppa, and told him, "Twelve gon' show up askin' questions, and I ain't about to be here for that shit."

"I'ma stay here with bro n'em. If twelve question me, then I'ma tell them bitches I ain't see shit," Poppa let him know.

116

"A'ight. Hit me up and let me know what's goin' on with Chedda as soon you know somethin'."

"ASAP."

Ace gave Poppa a thug-hug before he hurried out to the SUV. "Take me back to the hood so I can get my whip," he instructed.

As Sly pulled off the hospital grounds, he glanced over at Ace and asked, "You a'ight, G?"

"I gotta down that pussy-ass nigga, Stone. Till then, he's just gonna keep sendin' shooters at us. And I can't have him killin' any more of my brothas off."

"Yeah, I feel you. Plus, all the shootouts are keepin' the hood hot. And we can't move work like that. Definitely not with that dirty-ass cop Lucas sweatin' the hood the way he's been, tryin' to get mu'fuckas to snitch on us and shit."

"In between Stone and Lucas, I'ont know which one of 'em want my ass gone from our hood most," Ace scoffed.

Sly braked at a stoplight on 12th and North Street, hand rested on the TEC-9 in his lap. "Just don't let either one of 'em catch you slippin' in these streets."

"It's either me or them. And I ain't ready to give up my life yet."

"None of us is ready for that shit just yet...feel me?" said Sly as he pulled off with traffic once the light turned green.

"Yeah, I feel you, my nigga." Ace glanced into the rearview mirror and saw the blood painted all over his backseat. He hoped Chedda would live to see another day.

Soon thereafter, they made it back to the hood. There were police cars on heavy patrol following the shootout.

Sly pulled up beside Ace's whip, then the two shook up and planned to meet later. Ace exited the SUV, then Sly pulled off.

As Ace slid behind the wheel, he heard his phone ringing. He grabbed it and saw the caller was Mika. He was sure she overheard the gunshots once the shootout started. *Sis ass has to be worried to death about a nigga right now,* Ace contemplated. For all she knew, he could have been shot to death. He answered the call.

"Ace?!" Mika said, sounding worried.

"Yeah, sis, it's me," Ace replied while he sat in the parked car with the stick in his lap.

"Are you alright, bro?"

"Yeah, I'm a'ight. But hoe-ass niggas popped Bookie and Chedda. Had to rush bro n'em to the hospital. Boo only got popped in the arm, so he should be good. But Chedda was popped in the stomach, and his ass was bleedin' bad." Ace's head was on the swivel for cops and opps.

"They're gonna be okay, or what?"

"I left 'em at the hospital with Poppa, so I won't know shit 'til he hit me up," Ace told her.

"Okay. Well, a toddler girl was killed by a stray bullet," she informed.

"Damn." Ace felt remorse for the toddler. *Bullets don't have names on 'em*, he mused.

"Ace, you need to take your ass straight home to Paris and your son for now," Mika urged.

"I will, sis," Ace assured her before ending the call.

During the ride to the crib, Ace watched his six in the rearview mirror, gripping the switch in his lap. Once he made it to the apartment complex, he pulled his Infiniti into the parking lot and parked beside Paris's Honda. Ace stepped out the car with his Glock in hand and held it at his side, keeping the barrel downward as he tracked towards the entrance of the complex. Before entering, he concealed the switch on his waist.

Once inside their apartment, Ace locked the door behind himself. He went directly to the bedroom without stopping to say a word to Paris, who was in the kitchen. He put away his gun and bankroll inside the dresser drawer, then removed his Cartier frames, Cuban link necklace and Rolex watch, which he set atop the dresser.

"Ace," Paris called out from the kitchen. "Your ass better have brought the Pull-Ups for your son, since it took you so damn long to..." Her words were caught in her throat when she entered their bedroom and saw Ace covered in blood. "W-what the hell happened?"

Ace pulled off the bloodied Gucci polo shirt. "Bitch-ass niggas popped Chedda n'em," he muttered as he kicked off his blood-speckled Gucci sneakers.

"Oh, my God! Is everyone okay?"

"We rushed 'em to Froedtert Hospital, but I got outta there before I could find out anything." He stepped out of his bloodstained Balmain jeans. "Look, call Chedda's BM. Let her know what's up. I'm sure Nett is gonna be a mess, and I'ont feel like dealin' with that shit right now."

"Okay, bae, I'll go and call her." Paris hurried out to retrieve her iPhone in order to call Chedda's baby mama and break the news to her. She was cool with Antoinette and felt bad to have to tell her the father of her kids was in the hospital after being shot. Paris dreaded one day she would get a similar call about Ace, so she understood how Antoinette would feel.

While he showered himself with bleach, plenty of shit went through his mind as he scrubbed off the blood and gunpowder before bathing. Staying out of prison and a grave by any means was on his mind, wanting to live a better life had money on his mind, needing to get at Stone had murder his mind and more than anything, whether or not Chedda would live weighed heavily on his mind. One thing for sure, he didn't mind the ups and downs because they were part of the game.

Subsequent to his shower, Ace was back in the bedroom. Paris let him know that she talked with Antoinette, and she was on her way to the hospital to see how Chedda was doing. While Paris lay in bed, Ace set on the edge of the bed finna *FaceTime* Poppa. He noticed there were plenty of texts, notifications and missed calls, but didn't bother to check any of it. Instead, Ace made his call.

"Any news on Chedda?" Ace asked once Poppa appeared on screen, who was standing outside the hospital judging by his background. He dreaded the answer to his question.

"Good news, Chedda's gonna live," Poppa told him. "He just gotta stay in the hospital for a while after the surgery and shit."

"I know how that shit feels," Ace replied, thinking back to his stay at the same hospital after he had gotten popped up a few years ago by Bullet, who he had killed. "Whaddup with Bookie?"

Bookie hovered over Poppa's shoulder and said, "I'm good, big bro. Shit is just a flesh wound."

"This crybaby-ass nigga act like he was gon' die and shit," Poppa jabbed as he moved the camera from Bookie.

"Fuck you, Pop. The shit burn!" Bookie said in the background.

Ace chucked. "Y'all niggas crazy."

"Look, twelve questioned us, too," Poppa let him know. "Told 'em we got caught in a crossfire and didn't see the shooters. Said they know we lyin' just 'cause we don't wanna snitch. I seen too much *First 48* to go out like that."

"They'll be back to question Chedda. I'm sure bro know the script."

"Fa sho."

"Listen, Chedda's BM is on her way to be with him, so when she gets there, then you and Boo can leave. I'ma go and see my nigga tomorrow. For the night, I'm chillin' in the crib with my bitch and son," Ace told him.

"Then we'll holla at you tomorrow, big bro."

After ending the *FaceTime* call, Ace buried his face in his palms and let out a sigh of relief. He was relieved Chedda would live to see another day, and now he knew how Chedda must have felt, when he was the one who was lying in a hospital bed with bullet holes in him. Ace loved Chedda like a brotha, and after losing Gee, he didn't want to lose any more of his bros.

Paris positioned herself behind Ace, wrapped her arms around his shoulders, and pecked him on the cheek. "I know Chedda getting shot is tough on you. At least he's gonna fine."

"You right," Ace agreed. "Listen, I want you to look for us a new crib somewhere low-key. Just to be on the safe side." He wanted to put up his family out of harm's way.

"Okay."

"Look, I'ma get some Z's. There's shit I gotta do tomorrow."

"Kay. I'ma go and put Adonis to bed." Paris could tell he needed a moment to himself. She slid out of bed, grabbed the bloodied clothes for disposal. She headed for the door, then stopped in her tracks as an afterthought and said, "Ace, sometimes I don't know how you sleep at night." She exited the bedroom on her way to tuck in their son.

Ace lay back in bed with his hands behind his head, gazing up at the ceiling. He thought about what Paris had said, and he had to admit, he didn't get much good sleep in between having street dreams and fed nightmares.

Martell "Troublesome" Bolden

Chapter 14

It was early in the morning when Paris shook Ace awake. She let Ace know she was about to take Adonis with her to the daycare so she could go to work. After pecking Ace on the lips, Paris left out with their son, headed to her job at the daycare.

Ace sat up on the edge of the bed and stretched out of his sleep. He had shit to do today. After Chedda had gotten popped yesterday and managed to live, Ace had to go and visit his boy in the hospital. He didn't know how fucked up the condition the slug Chedda had taken in the stomach may have left him in. But what Ace did know, killing Stone was priority, for he was the one who sent the shooters. And Ace couldn't wait until he had the chance to stand over Stone and leave his face destroyed.

Grabbing his iPhone from the nightstand, Ace noticed some missed calls from Mika and Kiki, which he ignored, and left some text messages from Savvy and others on read. He logged into *Facebook* and looked at his news feed. Ace saw there were people making posts, saying plenty of Stone's niggas were bragging about what they were gonna do whenever they caught Ace and any of his niggas. Ace just shook his fuckin' head and replaced the phone on the nightstand. He began to get prepared for the day.

Subsequent to Ace taking care of his nine and dressing himself in all-black and his Kevlar vest with no jewelry, he was finna head out. Ace grabbed his two phones and keys off the nightstand, and his Glock from the dresser drawer, then put the gun on his waist. He headed out of the crib.

Once Ace made it out to his car, he slid behind the wheel and sat the pipe in his lap. Pressing the push-to-start button, he brought the Infiniti to life. He put on some music before pulling out of the parking lot. Leaning back in his seat, he steered through traffic on his way to the hospital.

Arriving at Froedtert Hospital, Ace pulled into the parking lot and found a parking spot. He placed the pole underneath the driver's seat, then stepped out the car, closed its door and chirped the alarm. Once Ace entered the hospital, he stopped at the receptionist's desk and asked for Chedda's room. He made his way up to the room and when he entered, he found Chedda lying awake in bed, while Antoinette was seated in a chair at his bedside. The eldest of Chedda's two daughters, Londyn, was sitting in bed with him, and the younger one, Jordyn, was sitting on Antoinette's lap.

"Ace! Dawg, I was wonderin' if you was gonna come see a nigga, or leave my ass for dead," Chedda joked once he saw Ace.

"Nigga, stop with the jokes when it comes to the folks," Ace replied with a chuckle as he moved towards Chedda's bedside. He acknowledged all of the girls.

Chedda looked over to his BM, and told her, "Nett, why don't you take the girls for somethin' to eat real quick." He kissed all of his girls before Antoinette left him and Ace alone.

"How you feelin', bro?" Ace inquired.

"Shit, nigga, your ass knows exactly how it feels to be layin' in a damn hospital bed after gettin' popped. This shit don't feel good." It was Chedda's first time suffering a bullet wound.

"True." Ace knew the feeling all too well from when the roles were reversed. "Damn, Chedda, I'm glad your fool-ass still with us. Don't wanna lose another one of my brothas."

Chedda winced in pain as he sat up in bed with Ace's assistance. "Yeah, I'm a'ight. Mu'fuckas had to take a damn .9-millimeter slug outta me, it fucked up my insides. Now I gotta walk around for a while wearin' this bitch-ass shit-bag." His frustration was evident.

"My nigga, at least your ass ain't in a body-bag."

"And Stone n'em weak ass gonna regret I ain't, on Gee," Chedda vowed.

"Look, that nigga Stone need to be whacked. But his ass has barely come through the hood since we've been beefin'. Somehow, we gotta find that nigga ASAP, 'cause he's been doin' the most and fuckin' up our money and shit. With all the shootouts in the hood, twelve been on our ass heavy."

"Yeah, them fags came early this mornin', sweatin' me while my bitch and kids were here. Bro, we gotta put Stone ass down, before one of us end up gettin' bodied or catch a body and go to prison behind this beef. This exactly why I wanna go legit with the strip joint and shit, then fall back from the game. 'Cause I ain't tryin' to leave my bitch and two babies with nothin' before it's my time to go. Real talk, damn near losin' my life changed how I think about shit."

"I feel you, my boy." Ace sympathized with Chedda, because he himself had been through the same shit before.

At that moment, Antoinette and the girls returned to the room with food from the hospital's cafeteria.

"Damn, bae, y'all back already?" Chedda said.

"Thought you could use something to eat, since you haven't eaten anything at all today," Antoinette responded as she sat the food on the plate rack. She placed Jordyn on the bed, who tried feeding her daddy. "Ace, thanks for making sure he got rushed to the hospital. Because I don't know what I would do without him."

"He did the same for me before, so now we even," Ace half-joked.

"Whatever, nigga!" Chedda laughed.

"But fa real, though," Ace went on, "Nett, Chedda is my brotha, so I'll do whatever I can for him."

"And he feels the same about you. Make sure you let Paris know I said I appreciated her consoling me. You better treat her and your son good, because they deserve it," Nett told him.

"Fa sho." Ace turned his attention to his boy. "Chedda, I'm sure you wanna finish spendin' quality time with your girls, so I'ma bounce," Ace said.

"The doctor said I should be discharged from the hospital in a couple days, then I'll be back in motion. So, you and lil bro n'em try to stay low for now," Chedda told him.

"A'ight. Listen, hit me up if you need me for anything. Get better, my boy. It's all love."

"Love, fool." Ace shook up with Chedda. Before leaving out, Ace said his goodbyes to the girls, and he told Antoinette he would be sure to let Paris know what she had said.

Back in traffic, Ace was on his way to see Mika. He knew the hood would be hot after the shootout last night, especially due to the little girl being killed by a stray bullet while playing. Although, he wouldn't let shit prevent him from going through there. It might sound dumb and the strange, but he felt safest in the trenches.

As Ace dipped his whip through traffic, his thoughts drifted into the air. The shit Chedda had said registered with Ace, but the main thing was he didn't want to leave his bitch and son with nothing before it was his time to go. And by Ace gettin' rich the savage way, he understood he was subject to lose his life at any given time, by way of prison or death. Therefore, he wanted to do whatever was possible to make life better for his loved ones.

Once Ace pulled to the curb in front of Mika's place, he parked and offed the engine. He pocketed his glizzy then stepped out of the car and headed towards the house. Upon entering the front room, Ace found Mika seated on the couch beside Kiki.

"Hey, bro. It's good to see your ass," Mika greeted him.

"You too, sis. Whaddup with you, Kiki?" Ace said.

"Shit, just chillin' with big sis," Kiki replied. She looked at him narrowly. "Heard about what happened yesterday on *Facebook*. I'm glad you're okay but, how is Chedda?"

Ace sat on the arm of the couch. "Just came from seein' him, bro good. He'll be discharged from the hospital in a couple days.

"That's good to know," Mika chimed in. "But it's sad what happened to that little girl. That's why I'm moving. I'm so damn sick of all of the damn shootouts and shit around here. Seems like you and your niggas are always involved."

Ace scoffed. "It ain't my fault these niggas out here stay hatin' on me and my niggas. It's really that nigga Stone. Dawg soft-ass mad 'cause we on top, and he want that shit for himself. And soon as I catch that nigga, on Gee, I'ma blow his shit out. He better hope I'ont catch his dick-suckin'-ass baby mama, Star, first."

"What do Star got to do with your beef with Stone?" Mika wanted to know.

"That bitch can lead me to dude scary ass, since he's hidin' and shit. And fuck Star, her ass bogus for fuckin' with that nigga anyway, knowin' he my opp," Ace breathed.

"I haven't seen Star in a minute. But Milwaukee ain't that big, so that bitch won't go unseen for too long," Kiki piped in.

"Right." Ace rose to his feet. "Sis, I'm finna get up outta here. I just came through to check on you real quick, 'cause I know your ass all worried about a nigga and shit. Here, send this cheese to Mama and tell her to call me." He dug out a bankroll from the pocket of his jeans, then pulled off three hundred bucks and handed it to his sister.

"Okay, bro. I'm going to visit her next week, so let me know if you coming with me."

"I'll let you know."

After leaving Mika's place, Ace drove around the block to the trap spot. He peeped there were plenty niggas from the hood posted on the block, wanting some more of Stone's shooters to slide through after the shootout yesterday. Once he parked at the curb, Poppa and Bookie stepped inside the Infiniti.

"I see all you niggas out here ready to slide," Ace pointed out.

"After we left the hospital last night, me and bro n'em slid on some of those fuck-ass niggas," Poppa let him know. He was seated in the passenger side.

"But I'ont think we hit shit though," Bookie chimed in from the backseat.

"Was Sly with y'all?" Ace wanted to know.

"Yeah, he picked us up," Bookie answered.

"Look, I just came from seein' Chedda. And fool want us to chill 'til he get outta the hospital. We gon' respect that. Unless we see any of them niggas, then on Gee, it's shoot-on-sight. But for now, let's get to this bag."

"Say less," Poppa agreed.

"A'ight," Bookie seconded.

Ace grabbed the half smoked blunt from the ashtray and sparked it up. He lowered the volume on EST Gee's track "Run N 2 Me," just enough to be able to talk over it, then grabbed up his iPhone and went live on *Facebook*. For a moment, he filmed them smoking on the blunt, while the music played at lowered volume in the background. Poppa flashed his MAC-10, and Bookie spread a handful of blue hundreds on camera. Once the track's course came into play,

Ace put the blunt in the ashtray, then looked into the camera and began talkin' his shit.

"I know y'all heard about the lil shit that happened to my nigga, Chedda. Bro gon' be straight, though. Savages are hard to kill. And best believe, we gon' get our lick back. So, for you bitch-made-ass niggas steady talkin' all of that savage shit, I'ma give it to you. That's on Gee." Ace ended the *Facebook Live* and then puffed on the blunt.

Martell "Troublesome" Bolden

Chapter 15

Moving the Infiniti through traffic, Ace was on his way to drop off Savvy at the nail salon. Even though there had been a stash spot installed in the car, he felt more comfortable riding with the .45 in his lap. But he did have his sack stashed away.

Arriving at the destination, Ace veered to the curb and the car idled with his foot on the brake. He looked over and told her, "Just hit my line whenever you're ready for me to come pick you up."

Savvy grabbed her Louis Vuitton handbag that sat on the middle console and said, "Ace, you bet not have my ass waiting long."

"Bitch, don't tell me what not to do, 'cause I'ma do my thang," he remarked, checking the shit outta her.

"Ugh. See, that's why I shoulda just took my car," she complained.

"Next time your ass can take your car, a Lyft, or walk. I'ont give a damn."

"Sometimes your black ass get on my nerves. Daddy, will you pay for my mani-pedi for me?"

Ace glanced at her through his Cartier lenses, and said, "Naw, I won't."

Savvy smacked her lips. "You petty."

"Sav, get the fuck outta my shit and go to your appointment." Ace grabbed his money-phone out the cupholder to see who was calling.

Savvy pecked Ace on his cheek before stepping out of the car. As she strutted towards the salon's entrance, she switched her ass in her fitted Dior sweatpants more than usual, figuring Ace would check her ass out. Before entering the salon, Sav peeped back over her shoulder and saw Ace was too damn busy talking into his phone. She rolled her eyes, annoyed by him not even bothering to check out her ass at all, as he gunned away from the curb on his way to the money.

Ace pushed the whip headed to make some serves. In between servin' dope and weed, his phone line stayed active with clientele looking to purchase product, from sacks of weed all the way up to bricks of dope. So much so, his line was liable to ring in a substantial amount of money on the daily. Therefore, it was imperative that Ace continuously switch up his phone line after a while, to prevent himself from being caught up on a Title II wiretap by the feds. So, once he made a hundred thousand off a phone, he tossed it.

Turning onto a side street, Ace pulled over in front of a rundown apartment building. He was there to make a serve to an up-and-coming dope boy. Once he texted he was waiting outside, the dope boy came out a moment later and entered the passenger's side of the car, and he couldn't help but notice the switch lying in Ace's lap. Ace served the dope boy a nine-piece of snow, in exchange for seventy-two hundred bucks. Afterwards, he and the dope boy parted ways as Ace jumped back in traffic. He drove around servin' a few more clients before steering towards the hood.

Once making it to the hood, Ace pulled to the curb and parked in front of Mika's place. He peeped a white BMW 745 parked across the street. *Whose shit is that?* Ace wondered. He pocketed his glizzy, then stepped out of the car and strolled towards the house.

Upon entering, Ace found a nigga he was unfamiliar with, sitting on the couch smoking a blunt in the front room. The nigga was tall, light-skinned and muscular, with long braids, and he looked to be in his mid-thirties. The unfamiliar nigga was drippin' in Gucci from head to toe, and the diamonds dancin' in his AP watch was a sign the nigga must be papered up. Apparently, he was the one who owned the BMW. Ace figured he was yet another nigga tryin' to shoot his shot at Mika. As long as the nigga respected his sister, then Ace wouldn't have a problem with him.

"Whaddup with you? I'm Mika's brotha, Ace," he introduced himself.

"Money Mel. You smoke?" the nigga replied coolly. He took notice to the extended clip protruding from Ace's pocket. But he wasn't the least bit intimidated, because he had his own pipe unnoticeably under his leg.

"Hell yeah. But I'ont smoke that bullshit 'cause it make my nose run," Ace responded, smelling the weed wasn't the best of quality. He pulled out a sack of his loud pack. "I got that fire on deck."

"Lemme cop some of that shit."

Ace tossed him the sack and said, "That's on GP. The next time it'll cost you."

"A'ight. That's cool." Money Mel put out the blunt he was smoking in the ashtray, and then began rolling up the zaza Ace had given him.

Mika emerged from her son's bedroom after giving him some snacks. "S'up, bro. Thought I heard you in here. Um, this is Mel, my friend. And that's Ace, one of my brothers I told you some about," she said as she took a seat on the couch beside Money Mel.

"Me and dawg already made introductions," Ace told her.

"Oh, okay. Boy, what're you doing here?" Mika asked curiously.

"I just dropped by to give you some money to send to Mama." He pulled out a sloppy bundle of money from the pocket of his Balmain jeans, then counted out five hundred bucks, and gave it to Mika. "And just so you know, I ain't gonna be able to come with you to visit her."

"And why not, Ace? Mama would be real happy to see you."

Ace sat on the arm of the couch. "And I'd be happy to see her too, Mika. But I just don't feel comfortable steppin' foot into a federal prison with how I'm livin'," he explained.

"Alright, bro. I'll let her know," Mika replied, sounding letdown. "Mama sent you a letter. I'll be right back with it." She went into her bedroom.

Mel lit up the blunt of loud, then input, "I know the feelin' all too well, my nigg. Them fuck-boys just had my ass cooped up in federal prison for a five-piece. But I did that shit without snitchin' on a soul. Feel me? Only been out for two months now and show me love, 'cause my name good." He puffed the Backwood, then passed it to Ace.

"That's how shit s'pose to go in the game. But niggas fuckin' up the game with all of this snitch shit. My big homie, Baller, in the feds right now doin' a twenty-year bid 'cause some fuck-nigga got jammed up and then mentioned his name. I ain't tryin' to go out like that," Ace said, then inhaled some weed smoke.

"Baller your big homie?"

"Yeah. He gave me my first sack and taught me the game."

"Me and that rich-ass nigga was just in the feds together. Yeah, fam' is mos' def a real one," Mel complimented.

"That's whassup. They need to free the real and keep the rest," Ace campaigned.

"Big facts!" Mel agreed.

Mika returned with the letter and handed it to her brotha. "Be sure to make some time to read her letter," she insisted.

"A'ight, sis." Ace's iPhone chimed a text. He saw the message was from Savvy and left it on read. "Look, I gotta get back in these streets. I'll holla at you later, big sis."

"Okay, bro. Stay safe."

"That's why I got this vest and stick on me for," Ace pointed out. He hit the blunt once more, then passed it back to Money and said, "Just get my number from Mika and hit me up whenever."

"Fa sho," Money Mel replied.

Ace exited the house and returned to his Infiniti. Before heading to scoop up Savvy, he dipped through the hood just to see who was on what. Seeing Poppa and Bookie n'em, he honked the horn and chopped the deuces at them as he kept rolling. Everything seemed normal, so Ace went on his way back to the nail salon. While in traffic, he bobbed his head to the beat of EST Gee's tune "Forreal," with the pistol in his lap. When his phone rang, Ace lowered the volume on the music, seeing the *FaceTime* call was from Chedda, and answered.

"What's to it, Chedda G?" Ace could see he was lying on bed rest at home.

"I'm just checkin' on you real quick," Chedda said. "I see you in traffic. Where you headed to?"

"Finna go and scoop up my lil bitch, Savvy, from the nail salon."

"Bet your trick-ass paid for her nails to get done," Chedda half-joked.

Ace chuckled. "You got me fucked up! Bet that bitch put it in my mu'fuckin' pocket." He braked at a stoplight on 20th and Keefe Street.

"Yeah, a'ight. That shit sounds good to deaf ears," Chedda kidded. "Anyway. Ask Sav about an update on the bitches for our club."

"A'ight."

"Was you just in the hood?"

"Yeah, but I only stopped by Mika's crib."

"What sis was on?"

"She had some nigga over there with her. And dawg best treat my sista right, or I'ma treat his ass," Ace added.

"Fa sho," Chedda seconded. He winced in pain from the bullet wound as he sat up in bed. "Shit."

"You good, bro?" Concerned.

"Yeah, I'm good," he breathed. "Just a lil sore from the surgery. And I'm still tryin' to get used to havin' to wear this weak-ass shit-bag. Niggas gotta die behind this."

"Don't trip. Poppa and Bookie n'em been on niggas' asses behind that shit. I just can't wait to catch that soft-ass nigga, Stone, then blick!" Ace stated and used a hand to imitate shooting a gun.

Chedda grinned. "Your fool ass with the shit." He saw Antoinette enter the room. "Look, G, I'ma check with you a lil later. Plenty much love."

"Never enough," Ace responded before ending the call.

The red light turned green, and Ace turned up the music as he dispelled. He arrived at the nail salon, then parked curbside. When Savvy noticed him outside, she found her way to the car and slid into the passenger's seat. Ace looked to see if traffic was clear before he pulled out into the street.

"Daddy, will you take me to buy some hair real quick for my hair appointment tonight?" Savvy asked. She was comfortable around him enough to take off her weave and let him see her braids. One thing for sure, she kept her hair and nails done, like a bad bitch should.

"Where to?" Ace needed to know.

"Any beauty supply store."

"Say less. Afterwards we'll hit up Playmakers." He steered the whip for the nearest beauty supply store en route. "Whassup with you seein' about the bitches workin' at our club? You know we finna hold auditions in a couple weeks."

"I know. But Toucan haven't been showin' up at the club lately. Soon as he do, I'm gonna talk with him about it," she assured.

Soon thereafter, Ace pulled into a beauty supply store parking lot and parked. While he remained in the car, Savvy went inside of the establishment. His phone chimed a text from Paris, and Ace took the time to text her back.

PARIS:

Your son wanna know will his daddy
be coming home tonight?

ACE:

Yeah. I should be there by 8pm.

PARIS:

We'll see you then. xoxo.

A moment later, Ace noticed Savvy emerge from the store after buying some packs of hundred-percent human Indian hair. As she was entering the car, Savvy's iPhone rang. She noticed the call was from her lil brotha, Dre, and she answered on speakerphone.

"Hey, Dre-Dre. What you want?"

Knowing Dre was on the phone caused Ace's ears to perk up. He pulled out of the lot on his way to Playmakers clothing store.

"Big sis, lemme hold like a stack, and I'll get it back to you after I make a quick flip," Dre requested, unaware that Ace was listening in.

"A stack? Boy, didn't I just give you a few hundred the other day? Dre, your ass better start getting your shit together, dude," she lectured.

Dre let out a sharp breath, sounding annoyed. "Man, you gon' gimme the bread, or what?"

Savvy glanced over at Ace, who was now glaring at her. "Dre, I-I... Um..." she stammered, knowing how Ace felt about it.

"Yes, or no, sis?"

"No, nigga," Ace piped in firmly. "Work a job, serve a sack, or rob a nigga. Do somethin' with yourself besides askin' your sis for her paper, damn." One thing he couldn't stand was a leaching-ass nigga.

"Savvy, why the fuck you got me on speakerphone! And while you around that bi—" Dre's words were cut once Savvy immediately took the phone off speaker before her lil brotha could say some shit Ace took offense to. She knew they didn't really like each other.

"Look, bro. I'll call you later," Savvy told Dre before ending the call. She looked at Ace. "Dude, you didn't even have to come for my lil brotha like that. You do too much," she muttered.

Ace shook his fuckin' head. "Sav, all I'm sayin' is lil dawg gotta learn how to get it on his own in these streets. I respect that you look out for him, but he can't run to you every damn time he goes broke. Your ass ain't strippin' and turnin' tricks for no nigga but me."

"So, now you pimpin' me, Ace?" She eyed him through slits.

"I'ont even mean it like that. I'm just sayin' you my bitch, not his. Start lettin' your lil bro stand on his own two feet, like a man," Ace advised her.

Savvy had to admit he was right. "Kay, daddy. You right."

"I know I am. Now, baby, go ahead and get a nigga dick right," Ace encouraged her.

With no words, Savvy grabbed the gun out of his lap and placed it beneath his seat. She then unbuckled Ace's Gucci belt and pulled his soft dick out of his Off-White jeans. While Ace leaned back in his seat steering the whip, she sucked his dick to hardness. As she flicked her pierced tongue over the tip of his joint, she jacked its base in her manicured hands. He braked at a stoplight then rested his head back against the headrest and watched her chew him. Savvy didn't care if someone looked in the car while she sucked him up.

"Damn, Sav, your lil bad ass suckin' the shit outta this dick," Ace groaned. He enjoyed the feel of her full lips wrapped around his piece. The way she took his dick out of her mouth, then spit on it and licked on it had him in a trance.

Once the light flipped green, Ace pulled off with traffic. He was trying to prevent from causing a collision as he gripped the steering wheel while Savvy gave him sloppy-toppy.

"Mmm... Zaddy, lemme eat it up," Sav purred. She put both hands on his dick and massaged it. Then she deep throated him and sucked him up like a slut. This caused Ace to bust a nut and she swallowed it then licked his dick clean.

Afterwards, Ace looked into her eyes with a smirk, and said, "Your head is *savage!*"

Following the drive, they made it to Playmakers. Ace found a spot in the parking lot and reversed the Infiniti into it. He put the pole on his waist before he and Savvy exited the car and strolled into the clothing store. Ace picked out a couple of matching outfits for himself and his son, with the help of Savvy's input. While they browsed around the store, Ace's iPhone rang. He pulled it out and saw it was a call from Sly.

"Whassup, Sly?" Ace answered.

"Dawg, fuckin' twelve just raided our trap spot in the hood! It was Lucas n'em," Sly informed.

"What! Did them bitches catch some shit up?"

"Hell yeah. They caught Poppa with two pistols and Bookie with a few ounces of coke, and they took thirty G's. Plus, when they kicked the door, Beast-Mode attacked so twelve killed him."

Ace was heated as hell. "Where the fuck was you when all of this shit went down?"

"I was out checkin' in on the other traps. Once I pulled up on the block, I saw all of the police cars and shit. Kiki told me what had happened," Sly explained.

"A'ight. Find out what's lil bro n'em bail, so I can have my lil bitch go and post their bonds, ASAP."

"I'm on it."

Once Ace hung up, he called Chedda.

"Just heard what happened," Chedda answered, knowing why Ace was calling. "Luckily there wasn't much more cash, guns, and drugs in the trap than it was. Or shit would be all bad for Bookie and Poppa."

"At least it wasn't the feds that snatched up lil bro n'em. Long as they keep their lips sealed, then twelve ain't got much on 'em. I'm finna have Sav bail 'em out."

"You do that. And I'll hit up a lawyer," Chedda said. "Ace, this shit gon' have the hood hot for a minute, so we need to stay low."

"Fa sho," Ace agreed. "And let's chill with all of this talkin' on the phone for now."

"Enough said." Once they disconnected the call, Ace already had it in mind to switch up his phone ASAP, just in case his was tapped.

"Sav, let's pay for this shit and bounce," Ace told her.

"Is everything okay?" Savvy could tell he was shook.

"We gotta go and bail out two of my lil niggas real quick. I'll be waitin' in the whip."

"Okay." She headed to pay for the clothes and shoes.

As they were in traffic on their way to post bail, Ace couldn't think straight after learning about the raid. And he wasn't surprised that Lucas's crooked ass had parts in it. He was pissed the fuck boys had killed Gee's dog, Beast-Mode. Fortunately, they didn't fuck around and kill Poppa and Bookie, but arrested them instead. Ace knew both of his lil bros needed to be bonded out and suited with a paid lawyer in order to fight their cases. He introspectively said, *Shit, all lil bro n'em gotta do is stick to the code.*

Martell "Troublesome" Bolden

Chapter 16

In a suburbia neighborhood located nearly an hour away from the inner city, Chedda and his family lived in a brownstone. And Ace understood why Chedda lived there, because Ace was finna move his own family someplace put up in order to keep them out of harm's way. He was there to scoop Chedda up so they could go to the hood. Since coming home from the hospital nearly a week ago, Chedda hadn't been to the hood, and now he was ready to show his face.

While sitting in the Infiniti parked outside Chedda's house, Ace sent him a text message.

ACE:

I'm outside.

A moment later, Ace's iPhone chimed when he received a text in reply. He read the message.

CHEDDA:

Come inside real quick.

ACE:

Shit good?

CHEDDA:

Just come in.

Before stepping out of the car, Ace pocketed the Glock. He wondered why Chedda wanted him to come in as he made his way up the steps to the front door of the brownstone. Once Ace entered, he came upon Londyn and Jordyn, sitting on the floor while watching *Frozen* on the huge plasma TV in the front room. Both girls rushed him with hugs, and he was sure to hug them sideways so they wouldn't feel the bulge of his gun. Then he fished out a sloppy bundle of cash and gave them each a hundred dollars.

"Now what do you say, girls?" Antoinette said to her daughters as she entered the room coming from the kitchen.

"Thank you, Uncle Ace!" the girls told him in unison.

"You welcome." Ace smiled.

"Girls, go ahead and finish watching your movie. Dinner will be done in a little bit," Antoinette let them know. She turned her attention to Ace. "Don't be spoiling them like that."

"I'ma always spoil my nieces. How you?"

Nett sighed. "I'm fine. Just doing my best to put up with Chedda. Seems like since he'd been shot, he just been so damn stubborn. You would think something like that would ease him," she expressed.

"Look, I know exactly what he's goin' through, due to my own personal experience. Trust, bein' popped don't put you at ease, instead it puts you on edge. Just give him some time and he'll be back in the right mind frame," Ace expounded. "Where is bro at?"

"He's in the bedroom. Ace, make sure you don't have him out too late."

"A'ight, I won't." Ace turned for the bedroom and found the door locked. He knocked. "Open up, bro."

A moment later, the door was unlocked and pulled open, then Chedda said, "Hurry up and come in." He locked the door behind Ace after Ace entered the room. Ace noticed that Chedda had his twin Glock .19s, both fitted with thirty-shot sticks, a bulletproof vest, and some stacks of cash wrapped with rubber bands on the bed. He had his shirt off as he attached a fresh shit-bag to his stomach area. "Just gimme a sec and I'll be ready to bounce."

"Take your time, bro," Ace suggested, seeing Chedda was still getting ready. And he noted his boy was unshaven. "Damn, Chedda, you lookin' real rough. We gon' hit up the barbershop along the way, 'cause I can't have your ass out here with me lookin' like you po'."

144

"That's cool." Chedda pulled his T-shirt over his head, followed by putting on the vest. Then he slipped on a zip-up Balmain hoodie.

Ace could read that Chedda was on edge, this would be the first time Chedda stepped foot back into the streets, since coming home from the hospital and being on bed rest for close to a week. But Ace knew it wasn't shit for a street nigga to get right back into the street life. He asked, "What's really on your mind, my boy?"

"I'ont know about you, but all of the shit goin' down in the streets got me to thinkin'. In between twelve and opps comin' for us, we gotta move better if we gonna last. 'Cause I ain't tryin' to fuck around and go to prison or lose my life due to bein' caught lackin'," Chedda expressed.

"I feel you, bro. Shit has been real crazy in the streets lately with the beef and raid takin' place. We'll eventually smoke Stone and end some of the beef. But for now, we need to make sure Pop and Boo are good after bein' caught up in that raid. This is the type of shit that comes with the street life, niggas just gotta stand tall and never fold," Ace expounded.

"Fa sho. Speakin' on lil bro n'em, it's good you had 'em bonded out ASAP. And I already paid a lawyer to take on their cases."

"And lil bro n'em told me some niggas from the hood feel some type of way in the county jail about us, so I told him to have them to call me."

"I'ont talk to a lot of niggas, but they still the bros. At least Poppa and Bookie know fa sho we got their backs, no matter what. What we don't need is to go out like Baller, with niggas close to us snitchin' 'cause they don't feel the need to repay us with loyalty."

"We don't gotta worry about that type of shit, 'cause lil bro n'em solid," Ace assured. "As for Baller, remember the nigga I told you Mika had at her crib the other day? His name's Money Mel. And he claims he was just in the feds with the big homie, Baller."

"I heard about a nigga by the name of Money Mel before. Word is he was the plug back before he got indicted," Chedda informed. He put on his chain with the bust-down cross pendant and his Rolly watch.

"The nigga seemed valid. And he was pushin' a new BMW, so apparently his money right somehow. It's just hard to trust niggas in this game. I'ont even trust Phat like that, and he was Baller's main man and shit."

"True. Let's just hope this nigga Money Mel is valid." Chedda positioned his guns on his waist. He headed into the front room with Ace trailing. "Nett, I'm finna bounce. Londyn and Jordyn, c'mere. Listen, I promise I'll be back home later," he told them. Chedda was sure to give Antoinette and his daughters hugs and kisses. Afterwards, he and Ace left.

In traffic, Ace steered the Infiniti towards their usual barbershop, while Chedda sat in the passenger's seat, mixing up a soda bottle of dirty Sprite as rap music played in the background. They both rode with their pipes in their laps. Searching for some napkins to clean up a spill, Chedda took a look in the middle console, and he came across the letter from Gale.

"Bro, who the hell's writin' you from the feds?" Chedda inquired curiously.

"That's my moms. She finna come home soon," Ace told him.

"Thought you didn't fuck with your moms like that?" Chedda was aware of the strained relationship Ace had with Gale.

"Ever since Gee got killed, me and her been talkin' on the phone lately. I just wanna give her a chance to be in my son's life when she comes home, since she was never in mine. Damn, my mama locked up and pops got popped up, that shit got me fucked up." Ace laughed it off to keep from crying.

Chedda poured up some of the purple syrup. "Trust, I know how it feels to grow up without parents. That's exactly why I do my all to make sure me and Nett are the best parents we can be to our babies."

"And I'm the same way when it comes to Paris and our son. I'ont give a fuck about how much I be in these streets, I'll never be a deadbeat dad, like most niggas out here. Think about it, how the fuck are niggas out here gettin' all this money, and don't even take care of their lil ones? But they'll cash out on some ratchet-ass bitch. I'ont respect those type of niggas. I know I be fuckin' off on my BM, but I still take care of her and my son 'cause I love 'em," Ace voiced with conviction. He braked at a stoplight on 27th and Brown Street.

"On Gee, that's some real nigga shit, Ace," Chedda condoned. He sipped on the drank, then passed it to his boy. "And it ain't too many real niggas like us still alive or free. This is why it's a must we hustle, stack, pray, and stay outta the way."

"You right about that, Chedda. It's on us to do what we can to make it out of the trenches before they claim us too." Ace turned up the bottle to his lips with thoughts of knowing he was one of the last of a dying breed.

The light flipped green, and Ace dispelled with traffic, driving the speed limit. While Chedda checked the rearview mirror for anything amiss, he spotted a cop car trailing. They were riding dirty with guns and drugs, and them being young and Black, riding in a luxury vehicle made them subjected to being stopped and frisked.

"Shit. Twelve behind us," Chedda pointed out.

Checking the rearview mirror himself, Ace continued to drive real smooth and kept his cool. "Them bitches always tryin' to catch niggas ridin' dirty," he snorted.

Chedda knew his boy well enough to know if the cops tried pulling them over for a traffic stop, then Ace would take them on a high-speed chase. And Ace wasn't willing to go back to prison under any circumstances, even if he had to go out bustin'. Luckily, the cop car just switched lanes and passed by them in traffic.

Shortly thereafter, they arrived at Top Of The Line barbershop. As Ace was parking the whip, his money-phone rang. Chedda tucked his twin Glocks, then stepped out the Infiniti and strolled into the establishment, leaving Ace to his call. Looking at the display, Ace saw the call was from Sonny Boy.

"Talk to me, my nigga," Ace answered.

"I wanna cop some more of that smoke," Sonny requested.

"Just pull up on me. I'm at Top Of The Line, on 27th and Atkinson Street."

"On my way right now. In a minute."

After killing the call, Ace pocketed his Glock, then hopped out the car and made his way into the barbershop. The shop was busy with barbers cutting hair as clippers buzzed, and the interior was designed similar to a man-cave. While Ace and Chedda sat waiting to get a haircut, Sonny Boy entered the shop, then took a seat beside them. Ace introduced Sonny Boy to Chedda, since the two didn't formally know each other. Chedda stepped away to get himself all lined up, leaving Ace alone to deal with Sonny.

"Sonny, how much smoke are you tryin' to cop?" Ace wanted to know.

"Lemme get a half-zip of that shit," Sonny responded.

148

"I got that for you. Just gimme eighty bucks."

"That's cool."

Ace and Sonny discreetly made their transaction. "Just hit me up for whatever."

"You know I will," Sonny Boy assured. "Have you hollered at that nigga, Phat?"

"Hell naw. I'ont be fuckin' with dawg as much as I used to."

"Well, his ass sold me a stepped-on brick that was no good. Been tryin' to get in touch with him so he can straighten me out, but he haven't answered. If you holla at Phat before I do, tell him to holla at me."

"If I holla at Phat, I'll let him know whassup," Ace said. "But check it out. I know I was the one who plugged you in with him, and since you my nigga, I gotta keep shit a buck with you." He could see that he now had Sonny Boy's undivided attention. "On the low, I been gettin' funny vibes from buddy. So, watch your back."

"Then why are you doin' any business at all with Phat?"

"'Cause I'm just keepin' his ass close, for now. And maybe you should do the same."

"Enough said." Sonny understood Ace was only looking out for his best interest, and he would be sure to take heed. For he knew niggas were quick to pull back-door moves. He was finna leave but had an afterthought and said, "And good lookin' on takin' care of that one hit for me with Forty. Now my clientele back on deck."

"What about your brotha though?"

Sonny scoffed. "Man, fuck dude. His ass talkin' 'bout he knows I had to have somethin' to do with what happened to that weak-ass nigga, Forty. And now he's actin' like he wants beef behind that shit. I told Blue he can either get money with me, or beef with me. It is what it is."

"Sonny, I know you told me you'll handle your bro, and I respect that. But if Blue bring beef my way, then I ain't never been the type to call off beef," Ace forewarned.

"I hear you, my nigga," Sonny said. He noticed a bad-ass, dark-skinned bitch leaving the shop with her toddler son, who had just gotten his hair cut. "I'ma get up with you. Lemme go and holla at shorty." He shook up with Ace before going after the bitch.

When it was Ace's turn, he sat in the barber's chair. Twenty minutes later, his low haircut with the taper and deep waves was crispy. He paid his barber fifty bucks, tip included for a job well-done. And Chedda was trimmed up with his long dreadlocks with the tips dyed blonde, pulled back into a ponytail. Afterwards, the two headed out of the shop.

"Now, let's get to the hood," Chedda said as they returned to the Infiniti. He entered the passenger's seat.

"I'm sure the whole hood can't wait to see your fool ass," Ace replied. He push-started the whip, and then pulled away from the curb.

It wasn't long before they were in the hood. Ace made a stop at the liquor store as Chedda had directed him to. They both tucked their sticks, before stepping out the car and making their way inside the store. While Ace headed towards the beverages, Chedda went for a box of blunts. As Ace grabbed a bottled water, he overheard Abdul excitedly greet Chedda and tell him it was good to see him. After purchasing their items, Ace and Chedda exited.

The two jumped back into the Infiniti, then dipped around the corner to Mika's crib. As Ace turned the car onto the block, to Chedda's surprise, there was a small get-together on his behalf. Mostly everyone from the hood were present, they wanted Chedda to know he was loved.

"Ace, why your fool ass didn't tell me about this shit?!" Chedda said. He felt good seeing all the love.

"'Cause nigga, I wanted you to see the shit for yourself," Ace told him. After he had been popped up himself, he knew how it felt to live through it, and wanted his boy to understand he's lucky to be alive. Especially after losing Gee to some gunfire.

Ace parked the whip, then he and Chedda exited. Everyone greeted Chedda with hugs and handshakes. Mika and Kiki was among the first to greet him. And the rest of his boys, Poppa, Bookie and Sly, all surrounded him with love and respect.

"How you feel, big bro?" Bookie asked.

"A nigga feelin' the love and shit," Chedda replied.

"You know we got love for your ass, my nigga," Poppa assured.

Sly grinned. "I'm still mad at your fool ass for bleedin' all over the interior of my new whip. Know how hard it is to get bloodstains outta leather?" he half-joked, and everyone laughed.

"On some real shit, we just glad Chedda's still with us," Ace piped in. "We can't lose no more of our dawgs. So, niggas gotta be on point in the streets. And I ain't just talkin' about with the opps, we gotta watch our backs for twelve too, 'cause they want us just as bad."

"Yeah, Ace is right," Chedda cosigned. "'Cause not only was me gettin' popped somethin' we need to take serious, but also the raid Pop and Boo had gotten snatched up in. I know this is the life we chose, but we ain't gon' let opps or twelve take us out so fuckin' easy. So, we gotta keep runnin' it up while we stay strapped for opps and stay alert for twelve. That's the only way we gon' survive and get rich. Feel me."

"Good lookin' on bondin' us out," Bookie said.

Poppa added, "And gettin' us a lawyer."

"Like Ace and Chedda said, we gotta stay ready from now on," Sly input.

They all understood it was survival of the fittest.

Reverend Johnson approached the gang. "Son, you're lucky the Lord feels like your life was worth sparing," he addressed Chedda. "So don't take it for granted, because I can't say the same about that innocent, sweet little girl, Sierra, who unfortunately lost her life instead."

"Yeah, I heard about that lil girl, Sierra. And it really bothers me that I was spared but she wasn't. Especially with me bein' a girl dad. So…trust me, Rev, it's bittersweet for me to still be alive," Chedda replied remorsefully. The news of little Sierra being killed by a stray bullet, in the crossfire when he was shot, was truly heavy on Chedda's heart. He had even paid for the little girl's funeral just to show his remorse.

"Well, I was told you were the one who took care of Sierra's funeral expenses. That was admirable of you. And I just want you to know as unfortunate as it was for me to have to bury such a young soul, it was a beautiful ceremony," Rev let him know. He had been the one to give the sermon during Sierra's homecoming, and it was one of the toughest burials for him yet. His eyes surveyed all of the faces of the young brothers standing before him, and he said to each of them, "You young Black brothers need to start cherishing your lives. Cease the senseless killings of each other in these streets over the root of all evil. Put the guns and the drugs down, before you either wound up in prison or dead."

"But Rev," Ace chimed in, "how can you blame us, when we're just tryin' to stay alive, and beat the odds of our kind dyin' by the age of twenty-five. 'Cause when I stopped fearin' for my life is when I started totin' a gun."

"Believe me, I understand you all seem to be against all odds. You have to beat the streets, beat the system, beat poverty, and beat racism. However, it's on you to find a righteous way to beat those odds," Rev laid out. Sadly enough, he was sure he would have to bury another one of those standing before him sooner or later. "Now, young brothers, take care." Reverend Johnson left Ace n'em be, as he went back to watch the neighborhood from his porch.

"Rev ass always preachin' to us, but one thing I can say is he always say some shit that makes sense," Ace commented.

"True," Chedda concurred.

After chillin' in the hood for a couple of hours, Chedda was ready to get home for the night. Once Ace and Chedda returned to the Infiniti, Ace push-started the car and flicked on the headlights seeing that it was growing dark outside, then pulled away from the curb. The two passed a blunt of loud back and forth as they rode through traffic. Ace yielded at a stoplight on 50th and Capital Street.

While awaiting the light to flip green, Ace peeped a familiar vehicle as it made its way down the street. He reached under his T-shirt with a photo of Gee's face on it and pulled out the switch and held it in his lap, then heatedly said, "You see this shit, Chedda?"

"Yeah, I see. Now pull up on that mu'fucka!" Chedda insisted, ready to put in gun work.

After bustin' an illegal U-turn, Ace and Chedda tailed Stone's red Chrysler 300C sittin' on twenty-four-inch chrome rims. While they tailed Stone's whip, he was oblivious to Ace n'em lurkin' on him. As Stone braked at a stoplight, Ace was sure to stay at least two cars behind, so he wouldn't be detected. He wanted nothing more than to catch Stone without giving him a chance to make any sort of get away, because Ace was hellbent on stopping Stone's breaths.

"Fuck you doin', Ace? Pull up next to the car so we can air that mu'fucka out," Chedda urged. He held both of his poles in his lap.

"Naw, I'ont wanna fuck around and miss the nigga, then have to chase him down in traffic and his bitch-ass ends up gettin' away somehow. So, I'ma tail his ass 'til he makes a stop. Then I'ma hop out on his ass when he least expects it, and get close up on him, you know that shit be graphic," Ace told him.

"And then what if the nigga duck for cover and happens to still get away?"

"You know damn well he can't duck these switches." Ace glanced down in his lap at his .45 Glock, fixed with a thirty-two-shot clip and a converter switch to make it shoot like a mini-AK.

"A'ight. But you already know you gotta shoot forward 'cause that bitch be glitchin'."

"Fa sho." Ace tried to get a good look inside of the Chrysler to see how many people were possibly occupying it, but he wasn't able to do so due to its mirror-tint windows. "Damn. Can you see if someone else is ridin' in the car with the nigga?"

"Yeah, I can see it's two people in the car." Chedda happened to make out two silhouettes through the mirror-tint windows. "But it don't matter, 'cause whoever's with him can get shot too," he stated.

"You know I'ma shoot Stone ass down and whoever's ridin' with him," Ace assured him.

Once the light turned green, Ace stayed on the Chrysler's tail as it pulled off with traffic. He wanted Stone to make a stop, and he would pull up with no warning, then hop out and scorch him. While tailing the car, Ace couldn't help but to have flashbacks of the night when Gee was killed. His brotha lost his life, and it turned Ace even more savage hearted. Holding Gee in his arms until he had taken his final breath, seeing the tormented look in Mika's eyes, in that terrible moment the only thing Ace had thought about was getting vengeance on whomever done it. And Ace had vowed he wouldn't be satisfied until whomever done it is not breathing. So, he would make good on that vow to Gee by making Stone take his last breaths.

After several turns and detours with the hopes of shaking any tail, Stone was still oblivious to Ace and Chedda on his ass. Ace cut the headlights as he tailed the Chrysler onto a side street in a quiet neighborhood, located far away from their ghetto. Then Ace and Chedda realized this was where Stone must have been laying low after Gee's murder. They were on Stone's tail, and he wasn't even aware of it. Once the Chrysler pulled curbside and parked in front of a handsome family home, Ace veered the Infiniti to the curb a couple of houses down the street, out of sight. A moment later, Ace and Chedda observed Stone step out the driver's side of the Chrysler, they peeped that he was dripped in diamonds around his neck and wrist, along with the bulge of an extended clip protruding from his waist.

"There Stone bitch-ass is now," Ace pointed out, gripping his switch.

"Hop out and go get busy." Chedda geeked up his boy to go for the kill.

"On Gee, this nigga finna take his last breaths."

Without further words, Ace slipped out of the Infiniti, and Chedda slid over the middle console into the driver's seat. With his switch in hand, ready for action, Ace ran up on an unsuspecting Stone, who was pulling open the passenger's door. And once Stone peeped a nigga running up on him, he then recognized it was Ace! Stone instantly went for his waist and upped the FN 5.6 handgun fitted with a thirty-shot stick. Ace and Stone shot it out to see who'd live to tell the story later.

Boc! Boc! Boc! Boc! Boc!

Blocka! Blocka! Blocka!

The two archenemies simultaneously let off rapid gunfire at one another, Stone's slugs missed and wildly strayed off as Ace's struck Stone four times in the chest. On impact, the slugs forced Stone backwards, he slammed back against the side of the Chrysler, leaving blood smeared on its red paint job as he collapsed onto the ground. Star, the passenger, had attempted to duck for cover but was still struck down by .45 slugs.

"This for Gee, you bitch-ass nigga!" Ace hissed, as he walked up on a helpless Stone. He found triumph in witnessing the bitch-made-ass nigga choking to death on his own blood and desperately chasing his breath. Ace's eyes glittered coldly while he aimed the .45 down on Stone's face. Ace permitted himself a thin smile as he squeezed the trigger.

Boc! Boc! Boc!

Ace stood over Stone and left his face destroyed. Once the fatal shots were delivered, Chedda pulled up and then Ace hurried to the Infiniti and jumped inside the passenger's seat with his gun smoking. Chedda skirted away down the street, leaving behind a murder scene. Now that Ace had killed Stone, he felt some vindication, although he knew it still wouldn't bring back Gee. Ace and Chedda rode in silence while listening to Lil Poppa's tune, "R.I.P."

To Be Continued...
Rich $avage 3
Coming Soon

Lock Down Publications and Ca$h Presents
assisted publishing packages.

BASIC PACKAGE $499
Editing
Cover Design
Formatting

UPGRADED PACKAGE $800
Typing
Editing
Cover Design
Formatting

ADVANCE PACKAGE $1,200
Typing
Editing
Cover Design
Formatting
Copyright registration
Proofreading
Upload book to Amazon

LDP SUPREME PACKAGE $1,500
Typing
Editing
Cover Design
Formatting
Copyright registration
Proofreading
Set up Amazon account

Upload book to Amazon
Advertise on LDP Amazon and Facebook page

***Other services available upon request.
Additional charges may apply
Lock Down Publications
P.O. Box 944
Stockbridge, GA 30281-9998
Phone # 470 303-9761

Submission Guideline

Submit the first three chapters of your completed manuscript to ldpsubmissions@gmail.com, subject line: Your book's title. The manuscript must be in a .doc file and sent as an attachment. Document should be in Times New Roman, double spaced and in size 12 font. Also, provide your synopsis and full contact information. If sending multiple submissions, they must each be in a separate email.

Have a story but no way to send it electronically? You can still submit to LDP/Ca$h Presents. Send in the first three chapters, written or typed, of your completed manuscript to:

LDP: Submissions Dept
Po Box 944
Stockbridge, Ga 30281

DO NOT send original manuscript. Must be a duplicate.

Provide your synopsis and a cover letter containing your full contact information.

Thanks for considering LDP and Ca$h Presents.

<u>NEW RELEASES</u>

C.R.E.A.M. 3 by YOLANDA MOORE
UNBREAK MY HEART by MIMI
SOUL OF A HUSTLER, HEART OF A
KILLER by SAYNOMORE
THE STREETS NEVER LET GO 3 by ROBERT

BAPTISTE

RICH $AVAGE 2 by MARTELL "TROUBLESOME"

BOLDEN

Rich $avage 2

BLOOD OF A BOSS VI

SHADOWS OF THE GAME II

TRAP BASTARD II

By **Askari**

LOYAL TO THE GAME IV

By **T.J. & Jelissa**

TRUE SAVAGE VIII

MIDNIGHT CARTEL IV

DOPE BOY MAGIC IV

CITY OF KINGZ III

NIGHTMARE ON SILENT AVE II

THE PLUG OF LIL MEXICO II

CLASSIC CITY II

By **Chris Green**

BLAST FOR ME III

A SAVAGE DOPEBOY III

CUTTHROAT MAFIA III

DUFFLE BAG CARTEL VII

HEARTLESS GOON VI

By **Ghost**

A HUSTLER'S DECEIT III

KILL ZONE II

BAE BELONGS TO ME III

TIL DEATH II

By **Aryanna**

KING OF THE TRAP III

By **T.J. Edwards**

GORILLAZ IN THE BAY V

3X KRAZY III

STRAIGHT BEAST MODE III

De'Kari

KINGPIN KILLAZ IV

STREET KINGS III

PAID IN BLOOD III

CARTEL KILLAZ IV

DOPE GODS III

Hood Rich

SINS OF A HUSTLA II

ASAD

RICH $AVAGE III

By Martell Troublesome Bolden

YAYO V

Bred In The Game 2

S. Allen

THE STREETS WILL TALK II

By Yolanda Moore

SON OF A DOPE FIEND III

HEAVEN GOT A GHETTO II

SKI MASK MONEY II

By Renta

LOYALTY AIN'T PROMISED III

By Keith Williams

I'M NOTHING WITHOUT HIS LOVE II

SINS OF A THUG II

TO THE THUG I LOVED BEFORE II

IN A HUSTLER I TRUST II

By **Monet Dragun**

QUIET MONEY IV

EXTENDED CLIP III

THUG LIFE IV

By **Trai'Quan**

THE STREETS MADE ME IV

By **Larry D. Wright**

IF YOU CROSS ME ONCE II

ANGEL IV

By **Anthony Fields**

THE STREETS WILL NEVER CLOSE IV

By **K'ajji**

HARD AND RUTHLESS III

KILLA KOUNTY III

By **Khufu**

MONEY GAME III

By **Smoove Dolla**

JACK BOYS VS DOPE BOYS II

A GANGSTA'S QUR'AN V

COKE GIRLZ II

COKE BOYS II

By **Romell Tukes**

MURDA WAS THE CASE II

Elijah R. Freeman

THE STREETS NEVER LET GO III

By Robert Baptiste

AN UNFORESEEN LOVE IV

By **Meesha**

KING OF THE TRENCHES III
by **GHOST & TRANAY ADAMS**

MONEY MAFIA II

By **Jibril Williams**

QUEEN OF THE ZOO III

By **Black Migo**

VICIOUS LOYALTY III

By Kingpen

A GANGSTA'S PAIN III

By J-Blunt

CONFESSIONS OF A JACKBOY III

By Nicholas Lock

GRIMEY WAYS III

By Ray Vinci

KING KILLA II

By Vincent "Vitto" Holloway

BETRAYAL OF A THUG II

By Fre$h

THE MURDER QUEENS II

By Michael Gallon

THE BIRTH OF A GANGSTER III

By Delmont Player

TREAL LOVE II

Rich $avage 2

By Le'Monica Jackson
FOR THE LOVE OF BLOOD II
By Jamel Mitchell
RAN OFF ON DA PLUG II
By Paper Boi Rari
HOOD CONSIGLIERE II
By Keese
PRETTY GIRLS DO NASTY THINGS II
By Nicole Goosby
PROTÉGÉ OF A LEGEND II
By Corey Robinson
IT'S JUST ME AND YOU II
By Ah'Million
BORN IN THE GRAVE II
By Self Made Tay

<u>Available Now</u>

RESTRAINING ORDER **I & II**
By **CA$H & Coffee**
LOVE KNOWS NO BOUNDARIES **I II & III**
By **Coffee**
RAISED AS A GOON I, II, III & IV
BRED BY THE SLUMS I, II, III

165

BLAST FOR ME I & II

ROTTEN TO THE CORE I II III

A BRONX TALE I, II, III

DUFFLE BAG CARTEL I II III IV V VI

HEARTLESS GOON I II III IV V

A SAVAGE DOPEBOY I II

DRUG LORDS I II III

CUTTHROAT MAFIA I II

KING OF THE TRENCHES

By **Ghost**

LAY IT DOWN **I & II**

LAST OF A DYING BREED I II

BLOOD STAINS OF A SHOTTA I & II III

By **Jamaica**

LOYAL TO THE GAME I II III

LIFE OF SIN I, II III

By **TJ & Jelissa**

BLOODY COMMAS I & II

SKI MASK CARTEL I II & III

KING OF NEW YORK I II,III IV V

RISE TO POWER I II III

COKE KINGS I II III IV V

BORN HEARTLESS I II III IV

KING OF THE TRAP I II

By **T.J. Edwards**

IF LOVING HIM IS WRONG…I & II

LOVE ME EVEN WHEN IT HURTS I II III

Rich $avage 2

By **Jelissa**
WHEN THE STREETS CLAP BACK I & II III
THE HEART OF A SAVAGE I II III IV
MONEY MAFIA
LOYAL TO THE SOIL I II III
By **Jibril Williams**
A DISTINGUISHED THUG STOLE MY HEART I II & III
LOVE SHOULDN'T HURT I II III IV
RENEGADE BOYS I II III IV
PAID IN KARMA I II III
SAVAGE STORMS I II III
AN UNFORESEEN LOVE I II III
By **Meesha**
A GANGSTER'S CODE I &, II III
A GANGSTER'S SYN I II III
THE SAVAGE LIFE I II III
CHAINED TO THE STREETS I II III
BLOOD ON THE MONEY I II III
A GANGSTA'S PAIN I II
By J-Blunt
PUSH IT TO THE LIMIT
By **Bre' Hayes**
BLOOD OF A BOSS **I, II, III, IV, V**
SHADOWS OF THE GAME
TRAP BASTARD
By **Askari**
THE STREETS BLEED MURDER **I, II & III**

Martell "Troublesome" Bolden

THE HEART OF A GANGSTA I II& III
By **Jerry Jackson**
CUM FOR ME I II III IV V VI VII VIII
An **LDP Erotica Collaboration**
BRIDE OF A HUSTLA **I II & II**
THE FETTI GIRLS **I, II& III**
CORRUPTED BY A GANGSTA I, II III, IV
BLINDED BY HIS LOVE
THE PRICE YOU PAY FOR LOVE I, II ,III
DOPE GIRL MAGIC I II III
By **Destiny Skai**
WHEN A GOOD GIRL GOES BAD
By **Adrienne**
THE COST OF LOYALTY I II III
By Kweli
A GANGSTER'S REVENGE **I II III & IV**
THE BOSS MAN'S DAUGHTERS I II III IV V
A SAVAGE LOVE **I & II**
BAE BELONGS TO ME I II
A HUSTLER'S DECEIT I, II, III
WHAT BAD BITCHES DO I, II, III
SOUL OF A MONSTER I II III
KILL ZONE
A DOPE BOY'S QUEEN I II III
TIL DEATH
By **Aryanna**
A KINGPIN'S AMBITON

168

Rich $avage 2

A KINGPIN'S AMBITION **II**
I MURDER FOR THE DOUGH
By **Ambitious**
TRUE SAVAGE I II III IV V VI VII
DOPE BOY MAGIC I, II, III
MIDNIGHT CARTEL I II III
CITY OF KINGZ I II
NIGHTMARE ON SILENT AVE
THE PLUG OF LIL MEXICO II
CLASSIC CITY
By **Chris Green**
A DOPEBOY'S PRAYER
By **Eddie "Wolf" Lee**
THE KING CARTEL **I, II & III**
By **Frank Gresham**
THESE NIGGAS AIN'T LOYAL **I, II & III**
By **Nikki Tee**
GANGSTA SHYT **I II &III**
By **CATO**
THE ULTIMATE BETRAYAL
By **Phoenix**
BOSS'N UP **I , II & III**
By **Royal Nicole**
I LOVE YOU TO DEATH
By **Destiny J**
I RIDE FOR MY HITTA
I STILL RIDE FOR MY HITTA

Martell "Troublesome" Bolden

By **Misty Holt**
LOVE & CHASIN' PAPER
By **Qay Crockett**
TO DIE IN VAIN
SINS OF A HUSTLA
By **ASAD**
BROOKLYN HUSTLAZ
By **Boogsy Morina**
BROOKLYN ON LOCK I & II
By **Sonovia**
GANGSTA CITY
By **Teddy Duke**
A DRUG KING AND HIS DIAMOND I & II III
A DOPEMAN'S RICHES
HER MAN, MINE'S TOO I, II
CASH MONEY HO'S
THE WIFEY I USED TO BE I II
PRETTY GIRLS DO NASTY THINGS
By Nicole Goosby
TRAPHOUSE KING **I II & III**
KINGPIN KILLAZ I II III
STREET KINGS I II
PAID IN BLOOD **I II**
CARTEL KILLAZ I II III
DOPE GODS I II
By **Hood Rich**
LIPSTICK KILLAH **I, II, III**

170

CRIME OF PASSION I II & III

FRIEND OR FOE I II III

By **Mimi**

STEADY MOBBN' **I, II, III**

THE STREETS STAINED MY SOUL I II III

By **Marcellus Allen**

WHO SHOT YA **I, II, III**

SON OF A DOPE FIEND I II

HEAVEN GOT A GHETTO

SKI MASK MONEY

Renta

GORILLAZ IN THE BAY **I II III IV**

TEARS OF A GANGSTA I II

3X KRAZY I II

STRAIGHT BEAST MODE I II

DE'KARI

TRIGGADALE I II III

MURDAROBER WAS THE CASE

Elijah R. Freeman

GOD BLESS THE TRAPPERS I, II, III

THESE SCANDALOUS STREETS I, II, III

FEAR MY GANGSTA I, II, III IV, V

THESE STREETS DON'T LOVE NOBODY I, II

BURY ME A G I, II, III, IV, V

A GANGSTA'S EMPIRE I, II, III, IV

THE DOPEMAN'S BODYGAURD I II

THE REALEST KILLAZ I II III

Martell "Troublesome" Bolden

THE LAST OF THE OGS I II III
Tranay Adams
THE STREETS ARE CALLING
Duquie Wilson
MARRIED TO A BOSS I II III
By Destiny Skai & Chris Green
KINGZ OF THE GAME I II III IV V VI
Playa Ray
SLAUGHTER GANG I II III
RUTHLESS HEART I II III
By Willie Slaughter
FUK SHYT
By Blakk Diamond
DON'T F#CK WITH MY HEART I II
By Linnea
ADDICTED TO THE DRAMA I II III
IN THE ARM OF HIS BOSS II
By Jamila
YAYO I II III IV
A SHOOTER'S AMBITION I II
BRED IN THE GAME
By S. Allen
TRAP GOD I II III
RICH $AVAGE I II
MONEY IN THE GRAVE I II III
By Martell Troublesome Bolden
FOREVER GANGSTA

172

GLOCKS ON SATIN SHEETS I II

By Adrian Dulan

TOE TAGZ I II III IV

LEVELS TO THIS SHYT I II

IT'S JUST ME AND YOU

By Ah'Million

KINGPIN DREAMS I II III

RAN OFF ON DA PLUG

By Paper Boi Rari

CONFESSIONS OF A GANGSTA I II III IV

CONFESSIONS OF A JACKBOY I II

By Nicholas Lock

I'M NOTHING WITHOUT HIS LOVE

SINS OF A THUG

TO THE THUG I LOVED BEFORE

A GANGSTA SAVED XMAS

IN A HUSTLER I TRUST

By Monet Dragun

CAUGHT UP IN THE LIFE I II III

THE STREETS NEVER LET GO I II

By Robert Baptiste

NEW TO THE GAME I II III

MONEY, MURDER & MEMORIES I II III

By **Malik D. Rice**

LIFE OF A SAVAGE I II III

A GANGSTA'S QUR'AN I II III IV

MURDA SEASON I II III

Martell "Troublesome" Bolden

GANGLAND CARTEL I II III

CHI'RAQ GANGSTAS I II III

KILLERS ON ELM STREET I II III

JACK BOYZ N DA BRONX I II III

A DOPEBOY'S DREAM I II III

JACK BOYS VS DOPE BOYS

COKE GIRLZ

COKE BOYS

By Romell Tukes

LOYALTY AIN'T PROMISED I II

By Keith Williams

QUIET MONEY I II III

THUG LIFE I II III

EXTENDED CLIP I II

By **Trai'Quan**

THE STREETS MADE ME I II III

By **Larry D. Wright**

THE ULTIMATE SACRIFICE I, II, III, IV, V, VI

KHADIFI

IF YOU CROSS ME ONCE

ANGEL I II III

IN THE BLINK OF AN EYE

By **Anthony Fields**

THE LIFE OF A HOOD STAR

By Ca$h & Rashia Wilson

THE STREETS WILL NEVER CLOSE I II III

By K'ajji

Rich $avage 2

CREAM I II III
THE STREETS WILL TALK
By Yolanda Moore
NIGHTMARES OF A HUSTLA I II III
By King Dream
CONCRETE KILLA I II III
VICIOUS LOYALTY I II
By Kingpen
HARD AND RUTHLESS I II
MOB TOWN 251
THE BILLIONAIRE BENTLEYS I II III
By Von Diesel
GHOST MOB
Stilloan Robinson
MOB TIES I II III IV V VI
SOUL OF A HUSTLER, HEART OF A KILLER
By SayNoMore
BODYMORE MURDERLAND I II III
THE BIRTH OF A GANGSTER I II
By Delmont Player
FOR THE LOVE OF A BOSS
By C. D. Blue
MOBBED UP I II III IV
THE BRICK MAN I II III IV
THE COCAINE PRINCESS I II III IV V
By King Rio
KILLA KOUNTY I II III

175

By Khufu
MONEY GAME I II
By Smoove Dolla
A GANGSTA'S KARMA I II
By FLAME
KING OF THE TRENCHES I II
by **GHOST & TRANAY ADAMS**
QUEEN OF THE ZOO I II
By **Black Migo**
GRIMEY WAYS I II
By Ray Vinci
XMAS WITH AN ATL SHOOTER
By Ca$h & Destiny Skai
KING KILLA
By Vincent "Vitto" Holloway
BETRAYAL OF A THUG
By Fre$h
THE MURDER QUEENS
By Michael Gallon
TREAL LOVE
By Le'Monica Jackson
FOR THE LOVE OF BLOOD
By Jamel Mitchell
HOOD CONSIGLIERE
By Keese
PROTÉGÉ OF A LEGEND
By Corey Robinson

 Rich $avage 2

BORN IN THE GRAVE
By Self Made Tay
MOAN IN MY MOUTH
By XTASY

177

BOOKS BY LDP'S CEO, CA$H

TRUST IN NO MAN

TRUST IN NO MAN 2

TRUST IN NO MAN 3

BONDED BY BLOOD

SHORTY GOT A THUG

THUGS CRY

THUGS CRY 2

THUGS CRY 3

TRUST NO BITCH

TRUST NO BITCH 2

TRUST NO BITCH 3

TIL MY CASKET DROPS

RESTRAINING ORDER

RESTRAINING ORDER 2

IN LOVE WITH A CONVICT

LIFE OF A HOOD STAR

XMAS WITH AN ATL SHOOTER

www.ingramcontent.com/pod-product-compliance
Lightning Source LLC
Chambersburg PA
CBHW070526260626
47161CB00004B/1641